"I can't make out the signature. Is this some joke?"

"Not with a character reference from the Indian consulate. This is for real, April."

"Wow! I haven't the foggiest idea who . . ." Yet, even as I said this, I remembered the musky scent of cologne left in the fluoroscope room by a young guy in a silky caftan who smiled at me gently as he passed. I'd looked into those mysterious brown eyes and swooned, that's all. People did come to Dr. Shipman from all over the world for his cure, so why not from India?

"Well, I was curious enough to call the consulate, and he's a prince, at least a maharajah's son, the heir to a small state in northern India, notable for rugs and tigers."

"I could marry a prince!"

THE
YEAR
OF MY
INDIAN
PRINCE

ELLA THORP ELLIS

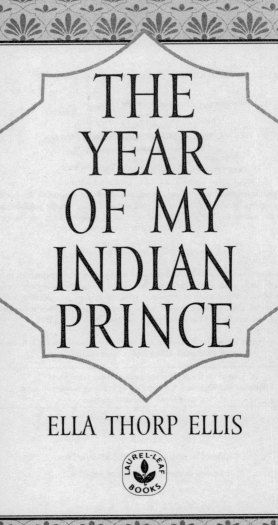

LAUREL-LEAF
BOOKS

Published by
Dell Laurel-Leaf
an imprint of
Random House Children's Books
a division of Random House, Inc.
1540 Broadway
New York, New York 10036

Visit us on the Web! www.randomhouse.com/teens
Educators and librarians, for a variety of teaching tools, visit us at
www.randomhouse.com/teachers

ISBN: 0-440-22950-2

RL : 5.2

Reprinted by arrangement with Delacorte Press

Printed in the United States of America

July 2002

10 9 8 7 6 5 4 3 2 1

OPM

For my granddaughter
Kristina Lee, who is
working to have a full life

August 1945

THERE WAS A FULL MOON, one of those blond California moons, lighting up the skies so you could hardly bear the beauty unless you were crazy in love. I sat on my side of the front seat of the car, hunched over and lonely beyond anything in the whole world.

Mike and I were driving home from our final summer swim-team party and he was analyzing my race. He'd won his heat by almost a lap, of course.

"The thing is, you tore out at the start, leading the pack, power to spare. Then, suddenly, midway you just gave out—or quit—didn't even place. Same thing last week. I don't get it, April."

"That makes two of us." Remembering, I shivered and my stomach churned. Each stroke had seemed to leave me gasping, but I'd kept going until suddenly I couldn't breathe at all. I could not inhale. I remembered starting to sink. But sheer terror must have saved me. Anyhow, I'd made it to the finish line, though teammates had to haul me out of the pool. I'd been having some trouble pulling myself out of bed in the morning, but this was scary.

"That's no answer," Mike said a little testily.

It may have been the moon or his tone or the way his jaw tightened, but something in me snapped. "Then go for a swim with me now—China Beach—I dare you." I knew Mike and dares. I only hoped Dad didn't mind. He'd just gotten home from the war in Europe so we weren't really scheduled in on things like curfews yet.

Mike was quiet a long time. "Okay, you're on," he said finally. He gunned his father's car, made a U-turn and headed for the coast highway.

China Beach was our beach, a clamshell of a rocky cove south of San Francisco with towering cliffs on three sides. The moon was shimmering out over the water, the way I knew it would be. An August moon. As we clambered down the steep path, I asked myself whether I was out to prove that I could still swim or that Mike loved me. Maybe either one would do.

I stood ankle deep in the surf and watched Mike race for the deep water, his powerful swimmer's body silhouetted under the moon, his face dark and intent. Then he dove in. It would never cross his mind that I wasn't right behind him. We were always challenging each other, and even though he was seventeen, a year older than me, I usually held my own. That's why he took my wiping out today so personally.

But now that I'd dared him and gotten us here, I

would just as soon forget it. God, it was cold. This was definitely not one of my better ideas. Maybe I'd go sit on the beach and wait.

"Hey, beautiful, come on in. It's great," Mike called.

I dove in. When I came up I couldn't get my breath for a moment because it was so cold. Then I struck out after Mike, and I swam myself warm. After a while I turned on my back to feel moonlight spilling over me in the dark sea. The mysterious and silent sea. This was no race, after all, even if Mike was still psyched up for one. He turned and beckoned.

"I like it here," I called. "You're out in shark country." He probably wasn't, but it sounded plausible.

Mike laughed, but in a few minutes he circled back to swim in with me. I was treading water waiting for him when today's fatigue, the shortness of breath, hit me again out of the blue. Oh, no! I had to swim back to shore!

Think, April, think, I told myself. Take it easy but get moving. Stroke, stroke, stroke. Mike's almost here and he can tow you in. Keep going until he gets here. Don't panic. One, two, three, okay!

Mike pulled alongside and blew me a kiss. I didn't say a word. I could yell if I needed help as long as he stayed near. I could make it.

"Hey, great idea, April. Refreshing."

I let a leg down gingerly to see if it touched the bottom. Not yet. Go, go, go, go, keep it moving. Then a wave lifted me, carrying me along as it swelled to a crashing release, catapulting me free. My feet touched bottom at last and I struggled to stand, waist deep, in the surf. I'd made it.

Mike came up beside me and wrapped me in his arms.

"Umm, you're warm," I said, leaning against him.

"April, you're my girl," he said, kissing me, and then, laughing, he sprinted for the beach.

"Heavenly," I gasped, wading through freezing water, heading for safe, dry sand as fast as I could.

Later, in the warm car, Mike's arms around me, his lips on mine, I was glad I hadn't said anything out there in the dark sea. He liked us just the way we were.

"Uh-oh, April," my father said two days later as he looked at the thermometer he'd just taken from my mouth.

"What is it?"

"A hundred and four degrees, kiddo. Time to call the doctor."

"Not much of a homecoming," I whispered. Dad had only been home about a week after four years in the army in Europe. As he said, we were just getting reacquainted. When Dad got back Aunt Gretchen had left for her home in Washington, D.C., after living in our apartment and taking care of me while he was in the army.

"Looks like I made it home in the nick of time," he

said, his eyes worried, as he patted my hand before heading for the telephone.

The doctor said I had a particularly stubborn atypical pneumonia. I had been in bed almost a month before I was strong enough to keep an appointment with a lung specialist. I still ran a low temperature and had a troublesome cough.

Mike went with me because Dad was working. We planned to sneak into a movie after the appointment. We hadn't been on a date for a month, and the privacy of a dark movie theater sounded good.

The specialist, Dr. Shipman, was middle-aged and six feet tall, with the piercing eyes of a preacher and gray hair parted precisely in the middle. "Well, young lady, let's take a look at you," he said after listening to my lungs and questioning me about my pneumonia.

"All I want to know is how soon I can go back to swim practice."

"Then let's take a good look," he said, his eyes holding mine.

I nodded and followed him into a little room that was pitch black. He flipped the light on what looked like an X-ray machine, but he called it a fluoroscope. He adjusted it so he was peering through the screen into my chest. I guess he could see right through me.

"Mmnn," he said, raising the screen and taking another look. "Mmnn.

"Turn around, please. That's it. Good girl." I was

getting used to the darkness, and I could see him purse his lips. "Just as I thought," he said, flipping off the machine and turning on the overhead light.

"What is just as you thought?" I asked as he ushered me out of the fluoroscope room and back toward his office.

"Sit down, young lady. Now then, there's a small spot of tuberculosis on your lower right lung, but I think it's manageable. I think we can help you become a healthy young woman again. Suppose you go along and dress now. Your father is expecting a call from me."

I stared at him, pulling the skimpy hospital gown so it covered me, suddenly embarrassed. All I knew about tuberculosis was that people in novels died of it. But I realized I wasn't well. It was almost a relief to hear him say so. By the time I dressed and recovered my voice he was on the phone with Dad.

"Yes, I think we could admit her tomorrow afternoon. You're right, sir. The sooner the better, for her and for everyone else."

I couldn't hear what Dad said, of course, but then this Dr. Shipman said right out, "I wish I could be more optimistic. I think bed rest will do it, but the cavity's in a tricky spot. Give her a few months in bed and we'll talk again."

A few months in bed!

Then the doctor was listening again.

"Yes, sir. Tomorrow afternoon, then."

Dr. Shipman put an arm around my shoulder and ushered me out into the waiting room. The other patients snapped to attention. Mike stood up.

"Aha, and what have we here?" the doctor asked.

"My boyfriend, Mike, Dr. Shipman." I was incapable of saying more.

"Young man, I think we'd better test you for tuberculosis right now while we've got our hands on you. Would you step into my office, please? It'll only take a moment. He'll be right out, April."

Mike gave me one horrified look. He went so white I thought he was going to faint. I guess Dr. Shipman did, too, because he took Mike's arm and hurried him into the office.

After the door closed behind them, I sat alone in the waiting room, still seeing that awful fear on Mike's face. Seeing his fear, I knew what I was in for. If I could have curled up and died right then, I would have.

When he came out, Mike still looked bad. "He says I could have gotten it from you already but he doesn't think so," Mike said.

And, believe it or not, that was all either of us said the whole time we were on the streetcar. Neither of us even mentioned going to a movie on the way home. I kept thinking how I'd been so sure 1946 was going to be my year. During the war I'd lived with Mom until she had her breakdown, then with Aunt Gretchen. Now Dad was home at last, and whammy! Tuberculosis.

"God, April, this is terrible. I'll call you, babe," Mike

said on our front porch, making no move to kiss me goodbye. In fact, he sounded mad, as if I'd exposed him on purpose.

We both stood by the door, not knowing what to do, how to leave each other.

Dad opened the door and Mike fled.

The next afternoon my father and I were having a last luncheon in the free world. In another hour or so Dad would drop me off and I'd be an inmate of a hospital.

"It's all happened so fast. I can't believe we're here—just talking—after . . ." I stopped so I wouldn't disgrace myself by crying.

"We'll come again to celebrate, when you're well," Dad said gently.

We'd come to the Golden Dragon, the restaurant where we'd always gone for Christmas and other holiday dinners when we'd lived together in San Francisco before the war. Until I was twelve.

But I was sixteen now and a tubercular. The war was over and my father was home, as I'd dreamed, but we only had this one lunch that was normal, because I was a freak, a contagious sick freak.

I was dizzy with the reds and golds of the tapestries lining the walls and the smells of ginger and jasmine. All during lunch I kept looking around, storing up faces and colors, the comfort of a great room full of

happy people [...]
wouldn't see again to[...]

If ever. Would I come [...] lanterns, something I
Dad on the phone with Aunt [...] hospital? I'd heard
ing the prognosis wasn't so good [...] last night, say-
Mom and she'd cried. And I hadn't hea[...]'d talked to
from Mike all night. [...] ther word

So I tried to fix it all in my mind, the big smi[...] Chinese families, the young couples in love, the delicac[...]
chopsticks and the happy jumble of Chinese and English. Dad tried to fill me in on his work making army
films in London, but I hardly heard a word he said.
And then, too soon, it was over! I watched in horror as
Dad paid the check.

"Well, April, it's time," he said, with the saddest expression I'd ever seen on him.

I nodded. He was waiting for me to stand up and
leave. Voluntarily. I couldn't look at him but I did get
up and, head high, marched out ahead of him.

2

BY THE TIME we arrived that Wednesday afternoon, I was so tired I could hardly walk up the hillside path separating the contagious ward from the main
hospital, even leaning on Dad's arm. I couldn't stop
shivering. My cheeks flushed. My ears burned and I felt
as if I were on fire. I started coughing, then choking.
Oh, God, don't let me choke.

I looked at my father, white as a sheet and staring at
me, and stopped coughing. He'd never been a man
who frightened easily. I must be even sicker than I
thought. "Not much of a welcome home," I whispered.

"Nope, have to do better than that, April," Dad said,
managing a weak grin as he opened the glass door with
the words TUBERCULOSIS SANITARIUM—CONTAGIOUS—
KEEP OUT stenciled in black letters above the visiting
hours.

"Wait!" I turned, still leaning heavily on his arm, and

looked back at the dry California hills. I breathed deeply of a warm breeze carrying the smell of roses and lavender. "All right, let's get this over with."

"You've been up quite a while," Dad said gently as we started down a long green hallway toward the windows of the admissions office.

The doors running along the hall were open, and as we passed each room a patient looked up and smiled, some welcoming, some with a sadness that made my stomach churn. I smiled too at each doorway and passed on. One handsome young guy waved and grinned. I grinned back.

They all looked comfortable enough, and most had been reading, which I loved to do. Bouquets of flowers stood on bedside tables. I was ready to climb into one of those crisply made beds and rest, to give myself up to the cure.

An immense blond nurse suddenly loomed before us, hands on her hips, tapping one foot, blue eyes icy mad. She glared at the stack of my records that Dad handed her. "Where have you been, Mr. Thorp? I expected you two an hour ago."

I shivered. Why did it matter if we stopped for lunch? Was I that contagious?

"Dr. Shipman said this afternoon. No specific hour," Dad replied sharply.

She tossed her blond curls. "I'm Mary Jane Alcott, assistant charge nurse, and I've been waiting to check you in so I can go home."

"My daughter's been coughing. We'd like to see her doctor, right away." Dad was not used to being yelled at.

"Tomorrow's his surgery day. He'll come up after," the nurse replied, more civilly.

"Tomorrow? Who's in charge today?"

"The charge nurse comes in at four today, sir."

"And until four?" Dad glanced at his watch, then back at the nurse, staring her down.

"I am."

"Good Lord."

"I have to sit down, please." My knees were buckling.

"You'd be better off in bed, that's what," she said, as if it were my fault I wasn't. Dad's scorn was getting to her, and I was proud of him. But tired, so terribly tired.

"Then hadn't you better get her to bed?" Dad asked.

"I am! Doctor says we'll try her in C two. Bed's been ready these three hours—sir. Follow me, please."

Mary Jane Alcott's skirts crackled with starch and the crepe soles of her shoes caught on the concrete floors, making a distinctive sound I would learn to dread. She seemed to me square as a block of wood and maybe ten years older than I was. Dad held my suitcase in one hand and cupped my elbow protectively as we followed her unfriendly back.

We entered a large and airy two-bed room, with windows all along one wall facing Mount Tamalpais. Mike and I had climbed Mount Tam the night the war in Europe ended, May 7, to watch the lights go on in the city below. Mike had said it was so spectacular because it was the first time we'd seen neon signs and streetlights and headlights since we were kids. Everyone drove with parking lights during the war to lessen the threat of bombing.

Everything in the room was painted green. That and the bowls of flowers on dressers and side tables made me feel that I'd wandered into a mountain meadow.

"My new roomie? At last!"

A hand with long red fingernails pulled back the curtain separating the two beds, and I saw Nancie Luchesi for the first time. She was probably the most beautiful girl I'd ever seen, and it was hard to believe she was sick. She was sitting up in bed, hugging her knees, and wavy black hair curled to her waist. She had enormous brown eyes, laughing eyes, and skin so creamy even the tubercular flush only looked rosy. I guessed she was about twenty.

"I'm Nancie, and am I ever glad to see you," she said with a light laugh, so joyous it made me smile, too, tired as I was.

"We're glad to see you, too, Nancie," said Dad.

"You look like Sleeping Beauty," I blurted out.

"Put under a spell by some wicked witch. You got that part right, kid," Nancie said.

Mary Jane drew back the blankets and pushed a hot

13

water bottle to the bottom of what would be my bed. "This kid won't be in here long if you can't stay in bed, Nancie, hear!"

"Mary Jane, don't be grouchy, baby, please. You know I need diversion."

Mary Jane actually smiled. "Dino coming tonight?"

Nancie shrugged. "Who knows? We had a fight."

"Again? What about?"

Nancie shrugged again, this time sighing deeply.

"Where should my daughter change? She needs to be in bed," Dad snapped.

"Use the bathroom over there. No spitting in the sink. I'll unpack you. Middle bureau is yours. I bet you gave that man a haaard time again, right, Nancie?"

I took out pajamas and a robe and headed for the bathroom. But I left the door slightly ajar so I'd hear why Nancie fought with her boyfriend and maybe learn why Mary Jane was friends with her and already hated me.

Nancie's talk about her boyfriend made me think of Mike. I remembered again that dazzling night on Mount Tamalpais when all the lights came back on. Mike and I saw it together, part of history. The world was my oyster. The war was over and Dad would be coming home. Was that only four months ago?

And suddenly I knew that my boyfriend wouldn't be visiting me here. He was too afraid of tuberculosis. I'd never see him again. This was the end of the road for me. I huddled in the corner, and quiet tears, the worst kind, the hardest to stop, soon soaked my pajama top.

Now what? I couldn't go back out there crying like a baby in front of a new roommate, nor in front of Mary Jane. Definitely not in front of Dad. It wasn't easy for him to come home from four years in a war and have to put his only daughter in the hospital. I had to pull myself together! I couldn't do this to him. But I couldn't seem to stop the tears.

The door opened slowly and a new nurse came in, quietly closing it behind her. She was an older woman, fiftyish, dark and softly rounded, and when she put her arms around me she smelled of jasmine.

"Poor little one, so strange this new home."

Her soothing voice poured over me, and gradually in her arms I managed to stop crying. Then she washed my face in warm water, kissing me on the forehead.

"There, now you are so pretty again. In the Philippines we say a woman needs her beauty cry."

I nodded as she helped me stand up.

"I am Mrs. York," she said a few minutes later, holding out her hand to my father as I climbed into bed, dizzy with relief, glad that nurse Mary Jane had vanished.

"Where are you from, Mrs. York?" Dad asked gently.

"The Philippines. The Japanese sent us to prisoner camp. Broke my feet and killed my man before you Americans freed us," she said softly.

"And here you are, saving my daughter."

"It is a gift," she replied, touching the gold cross at her neck.

What was a gift? Her getting here or saving me? People always tell Dad their life stories, I thought, drifting off.

When I woke it was dark outside, with lights flickering on in homes on the hillside across the road. There were curtains around my bed. Where was I? A hospital. Dad was back from the war and he had brought me. Marin County. California. I made myself breathe normally. Take it easy.

Then I heard a soft male voice murmuring beyond the curtain. Must be my roommate's boyfriend, the guy who was brave enough to come here. Nancie's Dino. Out in the hall I could hear the tray cart bringing dinner. Smelled good. "Dad?"

"Right here, honey."

"Don't we end up in the weirdest places?"

"Well, we've got some catching up to do after a war apart. This place will have to do, I guess. At least we're together," he said with that great grin of his.

3

THE NEXT DAY, Thursday, Mrs. York gave me a bed bath, the first of so many humiliations, so many things I could no longer do for myself.

"You lucky," she said. "I so gentle, not rough like Mary Jane."

Mary Jane had already yelled at me for leaving the newspaper on my bed table when she brought the breakfast tray. She'd probably use boiling water if she bathed me.

Mrs. York divided me into three sections like a sheep prepped for shearing. First she soaped me down to the waist and rinsed, modestly covering the rest of my body with a sheet. Then she washed from the waist to the toes. I was grudgingly allowed to wash my privates. Finally she rolled me on my stomach and washed my backside, finishing off with Johnson's Baby Powder. Then I put on clean pajamas while she remade the bed with clean sheets. All the while she gossiped about the other patients on our floor.

After the bath, Nancie brought over an enormous scrapbook filled with pictures of her boyfriend, a pitcher for the Oakland Oaks baseball team. She perched on my bed.

"We've been going together for six years, ever since I was fourteen. Isn't he something?" Nancie asked.

Dino was tall and dark and good-looking, all right. But there was something sullen about his face. If Nancie was Snow White, I thought Dino was a second-rate Prince Charming.

"We got engaged three years ago, one month before I was diagnosed and dumped here. How's that for luck?"

If we were engaged Mike would visit me, I thought.

"But here I am, mildewing away in bed C one while baseball camp followers and Dino's mother keep telling him to dump me."

"But you're engaged, Nancie. She should shut up."

"She doesn't want tuberculosis in the family. Oy, the disgrace." Nancie threw back her incredible black hair and laughed. "But I'll give her grandchildren yet. Wait and see."

Suddenly the door was pushed open and Dr. Shipman, wearing a white surgical gown, stood frowning down at us.

"Dr. Shipman," Nancie whispered, her face going pale.

"You must like it here, Nancie."

She shook her head.

Dr. Shipman just stood there, his eyes boring into Nancie's. "Am I going to have to put you on complete bed rest and post a guard to keep you in bed?"

Nancie shook her head, trembling.

"Answer me!" he roared.

"No, Dr. Shipman. I'll stay in bed. I just wanted to show April Dino's pictures."

"Why, when he only pitched five innings night before last? Has to do better than that if he wants my Nancie. Tell him I said so. And get to bed before you tear open that cavity again. And stay there!" he thundered.

Only when Nancie was back in bed did Dr. Shipman turn his attention to me. He studied me for what seemed forever. I dropped my eyes and flushed. He waited until I looked up again and then he smiled.

"It's not so bad here, April?" he asked quite kindly.

I shook my head.

"Your cavity's small and there's not much striation, so bed rest will probably take care of it."

He sat on the bed as Nancie had and asked if I had any questions. I was so astounded to hear a doctor actually discussing my lungs with me that for a moment I couldn't think.

"All right, young lady. No questions, then?"

"Yes, what's striation? What's a cavity?"

He nodded. "Striations are tuberculosis lesions. When one breaks open it becomes a cavity and you cough up sputum, which is contagious. Make sense?"

I nodded again, thinking of the CONTAGIOUS, KEEP OUT sign on the door. Mike would see that and turn right around and go home.

"Okay, young lady. Anything else?" Dr. Shipman stood up to go.

"Wait! How long will I be here?"

"Do you hear that, Nancie? She wants to leave us already. Seriously, April," he said, taking my hand, "every lung is different, so different that when I meet an ex-patient on the street after ten years what I'm really recognizing isn't his face but the old X ray of his lungs. In your case, hopefully not much more than a year."

"A year!" I wanted to scream.

"A lot depends on you, young lady. Stay flat on your back and you'll get well sooner. And what's this?" he asked, picking up my copy of John Dos Passos's *The Big Money*. He hefted the book. "Heavy stuff. Not the kind of reading that helps a young girl get well. You need happy stories, lighter books. Toss it." And he threw my book in the wastepaper basket.

"Dr. Shipman, that's my dad's book and I want to finish it. Please, give it back. Now."

We stared at each other for a long moment before he bent down and retrieved my book. Then he walked out without another word. "Who does he think he is, the army censor?"

But I was mad at myself, too. I could have picked Dos Passos out of the wastebasket later. After all, Dr. Shipman had bothered to explain what was going on in my lung. He was acting like a dictator, but if he could make me well—and there was something about him that gave me hope—I could hide my books.

"Boy, have you got a nerve," Nancie said.

I was more than a little nervous the following Monday as we went upstairs to be weighed and fluoroscoped by the Great Man, as Nancie called Dr. Shipman. Everyone except the dying got fluoroscoped every week, so I was seeing about fifty patients for the first time. People from our floor leaned against the wall in a scraggly line, like refugees, talking with second-floor patients in their beds as we slowly moved past their rooms.

For most of us, this was the only time we left our rooms, the highlight of the week. Dad thought it was crazy making us stay in bed all week and then keeping us standing more than an hour for the weighing-fluoroscope ritual. But we loved escaping our rooms and it saved the doctors time.

Everyone was staring at me. Why had I let Aunt Gretchen give me her French negligee? The lavender satin clung to every curve of my body. I'd felt like a movie star when I put it on, but now I felt stupid and cold. The other women wore wool or quilted robes. Some of them started giggling, including Nancie, my own roommate!

"Why are you laughing at me?" I turned on Nancie, behind me in line.

She took my hand, still giggling. "Oh, baby, Mrs. York must have given the guys your measurements. Their eyes are bugging out of their heads. She takes them when she bathes us and passes them on to any man who says he's falling for us. Says she believes in love."

"In love with us?" I looked over the line of wasted, skinny men in old bathrobes, shuffling along in felt bedroom slippers. I compared them with Mike, city champion in the backstroke, remembered his arms around me, remembered his kisses. These pitiful specimens. It was lucky I didn't throw up.

"You'll start getting notes from them. Mrs. York brings those, too."

"Doesn't anyone report her?"

"Why? It's kind of fun," Nancie whispered.

"Oh, yeah? Well, all I can say is, you've been here too long." I was sorry the minute the words were out of my dumb mouth.

Nancie's happy expression drained, and I thought she'd burst into tears. The desolation in her face frightened me more than anything else in this hospital had.

"Don't remind me," was all she said, but I knew she meant that literally.

And I vowed that I never would again.

"We take each day as it comes," Nancie added gently.

We were inching toward the fluoroscope room, where two doctors stood in darkness peering at lungs: breathing, damaged lungs. Lungs that Dr. Shipman saw instead of faces, ten years later on the street. Lungs he remembered from week to week and year to year. Few people were coming out of that dark room happy. And they looked pitiful after getting weighed.

"What's all this weighing in about?" I asked.

"If you gain weight, they think you're getting well. If you lose weight, it's bad news and they bring you cream eggnogs—morning, noon and night," Nancie said, clutching her throat.

I'd noticed Mary Jane bringing Nancie extra drinks, so I shut my big mouth.

And I was next in line. A dark young guy with gorgeous brown eyes came out of the fluoroscope room and bowed; we smiled, and he passed along. He was wearing a green silk caftan instead of a faded bathrobe. I was stunned. It wasn't only that he was handsome and had huge, almond-shaped, laughing eyes. He looked healthy! After he'd gone I knew where I'd seen him before. He was the guy who'd grinned and waved the day I'd arrived.

"April?"

Someone was holding the heavy metal door open. My stomach churning, I stepped into that dark cave. The room still smelled of the musky cologne the caftan guy had been wearing.

"Bob, I don't believe you've met this young lady. April Thorp, this is my assistant, Dr. Clark. No vegetable, this young woman. She made me retrieve her commie book from the wastepaper basket yesterday."

Both doctors laughed, though Dr. Shipman hadn't laughed yesterday.

"Now see here, her cavity's small yet and infection's confined—"

"Too bad it's so near the air vent," Dr. Clark said in a soft, sad voice.

"She'll need strict bed rest, but for the moment—"

"Of course. Might want to try a frenectomy, though," Dr. Clark said, tilting the X-ray screen for a better look.

My eyes were getting accustomed to the darkness and I noticed Dr. Shipman nodding.

"Why is it bad that the cavity's near the air vent?"

"Good question, April," Dr. Shipman said. "The vent brings air to the lung, so when you breathe, it also moves the cavity. Here, want to have a look at your lungs?" he asked, handing me a mirror.

Of course I did.

At first the lungs appeared alike, and I felt wonderful watching my lungs breathe, watching my heart flopping all over the place. Watching my own self. "Oooooh, wow!"

"Breath of life, my dear," said Dr. Shipman with almost the awe I felt. Then he started pointing out a cloudy area in my lower right lung with little lines, which I could see were different from what he called adhesion lines in the rest of the lungs. And a curious little white puff—the size of a dime, as he'd said—that he called the cavity.

"Positive sputum?" Dr. Clark asked.

Again Dr. Shipman nodded. I knew I was contagious, but the words were awful.

"Seen enough?" the Great Man asked.

"Oh, I suppose so," Dr. Clark said in that same sad voice.

Dismissed, I walked unsteadily out of that dark room. In a fog I was weighed and measured, my temperature and blood pressure taken. I realized how exhausted I was. In the same fog I walked back downstairs with Nancie and crawled into bed.

All I could think about was my heart and lungs pumping away up there on the screen, and the little tiny hole down in the lower right lobe, no bigger than a dime, no bigger than a button. That was all that was keeping me here? That was making me cough and run a temperature and ache in every bone in my body? That little hole made Mike afraid to get near me? That little hole was going to kill me?

Oh, no, it wasn't! Not on your life!

4

"SO, KIDDO, how are you settling in here?" Dad asked one night after I'd been in the hospital about a month.

Meaning what? It was early October. The war with Japan had officially ended, and Mrs. York wondered whether it might be possible to visit her family in the Philippines now that the fighting was truly over. Mary Jane and Mrs. York split the day shift on our floor. If Mrs. York left, I'd be stuck with Mary Jane.

Dad came by after work most nights, keeping me in flowers and reading material, so why was he asking how I was settling in? We'd play a game of chess or he'd read aloud or he might talk about his army life in England. But mostly he'd talk about how his day had gone, writing and directing a film about a railroad, and I'd give him a blow-by-blow of how I'd managed my day here in bed C2. I'd grown up talking with Dad about everything, maybe because there'd been just the two of us.

We've been batching it together since he and Mom got a divorce when I was eight. We all agreed it was better for me to live with Dad. Mom has depression that's a disease, not just a mood. Dad says Mom doesn't need a psychiatrist, all she needs is a full-time maid, but he knows better. Mom says she celebrates one day at a time. At the moment she's in a hospital herself, which does give us something to write about. Her mental hospital has a nurse like Mary Jane and a doctor like Dr. Shipman, who, she says, thinks he's God. She also sent me a great red wool robe after I told her about the men staring at the lavender satin negligee.

So here's Dad, still standing by my bed, a bunch of chrysanthemums in one hand and a *New Yorker* magazine in the other, with this strange half grin on his face.

"Settling in, Dad?"

"Made any special friends? You know."

"Special friends?"

"You know, any beaux?"

I snorted. *Beaux* was a word only a father, only *my* father, would use. "Here? Oh, sure, I roam the halls and they follow me back to the ward and camp outside, night and day, waiting. Didn't you stumble over them?"

"In a sense, yes."

It was my turn to smile. "Oh, yeah? Next time bring your camera."

"Lord knows how he found my address," Dad said, laughing and handing me a long, thick white envelope. I turned it over and there was sealing wax on the back, embossed with what looked like a crown. The envelope had already been opened, so I slipped out the first of three sheets of what looked like parchment, covered in elegant spidery handwriting, like something out of Edgar Allan Poe. I shivered and started to read aloud.

My Esteemed Mr. Thorp,

Enclosed please find references as to my intentions and character. More information concerning me can be obtained by calling the Indian consulate in San Francisco.

I am presently a patient in the same hospital as your lovely daughter. I have been very desirous of making her acquaintance, but, as she is a girl of good family, have been hesitant to do so without first presenting myself to her father. Since I am confined to my bed and it would be rude to summon you, esteemed sir, I have chosen this means of communication.

Would you be so kind as to allow me to write to your daughter and to speak with her on Mondays as we wait in line to be fluoroscoped? I ask this with the possibility, if we should prove capable of existing together in harmony, of matrimony at some future time when our mutual health should improve.

I eagerly await a reply at your earliest possible convenience, my esteemed sir.

"I can't make out the signature. Is this some joke?"

"Not with a character reference from the Indian consul. This is for real, April."

"Wow! I haven't the foggiest idea who . . ." Yet, even as I said this, I remembered the musky scent of cologne left in the fluoroscope room by a young guy in a silky caftan who smiled at me gently as he passed. I'd looked into those mysterious brown eyes and swooned, that's all. People did come to Dr. Shipman from all over the world for his cure, so why not from India?

"Well, I was curious enough to call the consulate, and he's a prince, at least a maharajah's son, the heir to a small state in northern India, notable for rugs and tigers."

"I could marry a prince!"

"Only if you prove capable of existing together in harmony, honey. Not too likely."

I nodded. Not too likely. Aunt Gretchen's negligee was not to be trusted. But being courted by a future maharajah sure beat lying in bed wondering if I'd ever hear from Mike again. Or stay here forever, like Nancie. I could hardly wait to tell her. "Do you think we could—"

My father looked up from the map he was unrolling, considering. "His father is the maharajah of this state," he said, pointing out a mountainous area in northern India.

"Maybe we could be pen pals," I suggested wistfully, thinking of saris and diamonds and riding out on elephants.

My father pursed his lips.

"You could tell him I'm too young to consider marriage, but—"

"In his country you're on your way to being an old maid."

"Tell him I'm too young here, and besides, I intend to be a famous writer. But can't we be friends?"

"Friends? Well, let me think about this swain of yours while we play a game of chess."

I lost in a dozen moves, but Dad decided that, if he was firm about this being a noncourtship, no one should be hurt.

And so began my curious romance with Prince Ravi Bannerjee.

5

As it turned out, Nancie didn't even know Ravi was a prince. Only that he'd arrived almost a year ago with a servant who cooked Indian food right in his room and slept on the floor.

"You could smell curry all the way down the hall. Dr. Shipman sent the servant packing and told Ravi he'd have to get along with nurses and democracy like the rest of us. But Ravi was a vegetarian, and butter and meat made him throw up and lose weight, which is disaster for a tubercular. So they finally gave in and prepared him a special vegetarian diet. Then the Chinese patients wanted vegetarian meals. The cook threatened to quit so they had to raise her pay. You know the old man I call the Mayor of Chinatown? He gets a vegetarian diet. You should have been here, kid!"

"I wish."

"But now Ravi's found his April, he's happy and soon well," Mrs. York said while giving me a brisk backrub, her hands carrying the comforting if heavy smell of rubbing alcohol.

"Poor boy, across the world from home and family and strange to American ways. No one in all his life spoke to Ravi in elevated voice as the good doctor did," Mrs. York went on, patting talcum powder on my back.

It was late afternoon, after our naps, and my temperature was up over 101 degrees again. Most of us ran a little temperature, but mine was high and that was as bad a symptom as losing weight. So I was glad of both the rub and the gossip. I no longer minded Mrs. York giving out my measurements. Hadn't they gotten me Ravi? Of course, I wasn't sure who he was yet. I mean, I'd seen him during fluoroscope and remembered his brown eyes. At least I hoped he was the guy with the beautiful eyes. But all that was before his letter. BPR. Before Prince Ravi.

"What's he like, Mrs. York?"

"If I were young again, it'd be love at first sight. God willing," she said, touching the golden cross at her neck. I'd asked her once why she was always touching it and she'd said the cross brought her good luck because of Jesus. I don't like getting people upset about religion, so I let the subject drop.

"God willing? How sick is he? Does he have a cavity?" In the hospital we divided ourselves into those who had cavities and were, therefore, contagious and hard to cure and the lucky bums who only had lesions.

Mrs. York shook her head and gave my shoulders a last hard massage before she sat back on my chair, resting her feet. "He has bathroom privileges and this month no temperature. What he really has is the homesickness. But now, with flowering hearts, you will cure each other."

"Hey, I haven't even met him yet."

Mrs. York shrugged. "You will on Monday," she said.

But that Sunday my temperature soared over 102 degrees and there was a curious dullness in my chest. I was allowed to wash my hair on Sundays and, since I have horrible oily hair, this was a treat I looked forward to. I was terrified that once Mary Jane checked the temperature charts she'd decide I couldn't shampoo. Then I'd have to meet Ravi, a prince used to perfumed ladies in silk saris, with icky greasy hair.

So, in spite of feeling light-headed, I got myself into the shower before breakfast and doused my hair with shampoo. I had only to rinse it and then, even if I fainted, my hair would be clean.

I didn't faint. I finished washing my hair. I even wrapped a towel around my head, struggled into clean pajamas and inched my way back, bracing myself from shower to toilet to dresser to chair to bed. The beds were high, so I climbed on the chair and managed to step over, sliding under the blankets, heart pounding and ears ringing. For a dizzy moment I couldn't see anything but red stars.

I closed my eyes, resting, listening to my heart. Should I call Nancie? No, she'd ask questions—too hard—just rest. Take it easy, Dad always says. Gradually my heart stopped thundering. I felt profoundly grateful to have made it back to bed.

Outside my window two hummingbirds fought over the honey water in the feeder. It was going to be a hot day. In the hall I could hear the clatter of breakfast trays, the sound of Mary Jane's crepe soles on the concrete floors, laughter. Beyond our curtain the priest had come to hear Nancie's confession, and their low voices comforted me. Soon I'd be strong enough to brush my hair. I had clean hair for my prince.

I pretended to be reading when Mary Jane brought my breakfast and the morning paper, hoping she wouldn't notice anything.

"Little Miss Vanity's made it to the showers already. Expecting a heavy date?" she asked.

"Good morning, Mary Jane."

"Up you go, lazybones. Scrambled eggs this morning. Get them while they're hot." She banged the tray on my bed table and shoved it toward me. I watched the tray coming toward me with horror; the smell of eggs was nauseating.

I felt something warm flowing into my mouth, warm

34

and thick and tasting musty. Not vomit, but fetid. I reached for the Kleenex and looked. Clots of deep red, with more coming. Blood. Blood!

"Oh, God," I whispered, meeting Mary Jane's eyes. "Am I dying already?"

"Uh-oh. Lie back—flat—or on your side if it's easier. Here, that's it." She put a basin near me and soon I was retching blood into it.

"Just stay as still as you can. This is old blood. Getting rid of it will probably bring your temperature down."

Why was Mary Jane being nice to me? I must be terribly sick. I must be in mortal danger! I looked up at her double chins, the small tight mouth, into the blue eyes and found them—not kind, really, but worried. And why did she keep pushing my bell? What could anyone do? Could they make me stop bleeding? Suppose I didn't stop—what then? Was I dying? "Call my father," I whispered.

"What's going on?" Nancie asked.

"Hemorrhage," Mary Jane said.

"Christ! Don't worry, kid, I do it all the time. It only scares the hell out of you the first time."

"Yeah?" I hadn't seen Nancie spitting any blood. Was it true or was she just trying to make me feel better? Oh, Lord, I was just so scared.

Mrs. York answered the bell, and Mary Jane asked for ice and the head nurse. "And take the tray."

"Ah, now the temperature comes down," Mrs. York said, but I looked up and saw pain and fear in her eyes.

By early afternoon the bleeding had pretty much stopped. Maybe I didn't have much more blood to lose? It could start again if I so much as sat up. Mrs. York said so. I was lying flat, staring at the ceiling, trying to figure how soon my father might get here, when Mrs. York came in again. She was carrying the biggest vase of long-stemmed red roses I'd ever seen in my whole life.

"For you," she said, smiling.

"There must be some mistake." No one but my father brought me flowers, and he stopped at stands for garden-type flowers. Unless Mike had sent them? To make up for not coming or writing?

" 'Sharing your pain, my beautiful friend.' " I read the card aloud. And beneath the message was the flourish of Prince Ravi Bannerjee's signature. I kissed the card and grinned at Mrs. York. I was disappointed and pleased all at once. "Well, so much for Mike," I whispered. Then I said aloud, "Let me smell them and then, please, take some to Nancie."

"A love story from the movies," said Mrs. York, setting my roses on the bedstand.

"At least he sends Cary Grant–style long-stem roses," Nancie said with an appreciative whistle.

"And, in this movie, does the heroine go upstairs to

fluoroscope tomorrow and thank the prince for his flowers?" I watched Mrs. York closely.

"In the morning the doctor say. Very good doctor. Nothing to worry. You are in my prayers." But Mrs. York busied herself straightening my blankets. She wouldn't meet my eyes.

And Nancie said nothing.

6

MONDAY MORNING I woke up to Dr. Shipman's earthquaking voice in the hallway. I'd barely used the bedpan and brushed my teeth before he pushed open the door and came striding toward me.

"What's all this fuss about a little blood, young lady?"

"What fuss? I'm fine."

His eyebrows shot up, giving him a startled look. He sat down on the edge of my bed, considering me. Neither of us spoke for some time. "Your father was so worried he called and bawled me out for letting you bleed," he said finally.

I couldn't help smiling. Dad would have something to say about that conversation. But I had to convince the Great Man I was okay if I wanted to meet Prince Ravi Bannerjee at fluoroscoping this morning. "It was only a little blood and my temperature's down some. I feel fine."

"I see. Cool as a cucumber." He took my temperature, listened to my chest with the stethoscope, counted my pulse and patted my hand.

"All right, young lady. I'd like to have a look at that cavity, but I think we'll wait a bit. I don't want you climbing stairs this morning."

"No—please. I want you to see my cavity. I mean, you should, really. And I feel fine."

"So you've said, three times." He pursed his lips, as if considering, but in the end he shook his head. I hated the way his hair was parted precisely in the center of his head. Hated it! Who but a tyrant would get up in the morning and pick up a comb and part his hair—just so—probably even before his first cup of coffee?

"Please tell your father I don't go in for bleeding my patients." He stood up with a sigh and put his palm on my forehead.

"All right, then, let's get you stabilized, April. You need bed rest to keep that lung still, and that means no getting out of bed for any reason, young lady. Your feet are not to touch this floor until I say so, understand? Bed baths, dry shampoo, use the bedpan. No bed-hopping to take Nancie a book or add water to your flowers. No fluoroscope. *Complete* bed rest." He pointed a finger at me and, turning on his heel, stalked out of the room before I could gather my wits.

"What a low-down dirty rat!" I gasped after the doctor left. "Now I'll never meet my prince."

"Want to borrow my Dr. Shipman doll and stick pins in him?" Nancie asked.

"It's worse than a prison. At least you can walk around in prison. Tell the prince I'm dying to meet him. No, no, just that I want to meet him." And I started to cry—silently. I'd learned that here, or else Nancie and I would trigger each other's tears and the place would be knee-deep in misery. Who needed it?

"Listen, April, stop that or you'll run your temp up again. I'll feed your Ravi such a line he'll worship the ground you hope to walk on. Trust me."

"No, he'll fall for you."

"Nah, I'm engaged, an untouchable."

As it turned out, it was a long four weeks before I finally met Ravi. And a lot happened. First the Mayor of Chinatown, the nice old man two doors down who sent us See's chocolates, hired a taxi and left the hospital. He had himself taken home, but he was brought right back by relatives who didn't want him at home contaminating the rest of them. Nancie and I hated his family, hating them most because of the reminder that we were contagious. Nancie's father wouldn't visit for fear of catching what he called the lunger's curse. Neither would my aunt Gretchen.

And Mike hadn't visited once in the two months I'd been here. He'd sent one postcard saying his mother wouldn't let him visit because he might catch tuberculosis. He'd also invited me to his senior prom if I got out of "quarantine" in time. A week later he sent carnations, with "To the most beautiful girl in California" written on the card. I didn't know whether to laugh or cry.

Then Irving, the gentle man from Ireland in the room next to ours, got really sick. We'd smelled the sweaty-bloody-urine stink that comes with dangerously high fever and heard his racking, choking cough for a week. But his coughing tapered off, and Mrs. York told us he was getting better. We didn't hear his wife crying anymore, either. Nancie had even slowed down on saying Hail Marys for him.

Then one day Mary Jane suddenly came through, shutting all the hall doors. The next thing we heard was the squeaking gurney being wheeled into Irving's room and then out and all the way down the hall.

"Holy Mary, mother of God, he's died," Nancie said.

"Yeah." It seemed as if I heard those squeaking wheels for the rest of the day and into the night.

But Ravi and I were getting acquainted by mail and that helped. A lot. Once he got my father's permission to "court," as he called it, Ravi sent a letter with Mrs. York every morning. They were several pages long and often made me laugh out loud. He'd been reading a book where the heroine chased her boyfriend around the park for a kiss and hoped we could play that so lovely game one day. Did I think the so ample nurse Mary Jane truly loved Dr. Shipman and without hope? His family in India would bow at my feet. (Your family someday, he'd say.) He was learning to knit but "I hide the scarf under blankets so the nurses won't say I am pretty girl. This makes me drop many stitches."

And his questions!

"Now what are you laughing about?" Nancie asked one morning.

"Ravi wants to know if you make the love with Dino."

"None of his damn business. Don't I wish!"

"But you're engaged."

"And sick. And here."

When Nancie got that quiet, hopeless tone, I tried to change the subject. "He also wonders if the soul can catch tuberculosis."

"I hope not, but sometimes I wonder," Nancie said after a long moment.

Another day Ravi asked if my father would call on him.

Dad said, "All right—this once—but don't you kids get the idea I'm some cheap messenger service."

However, he didn't seem to mind carrying the books we loaned each other back and forth. He said he approved of literary friendships. Soon it was worth his life to get past Ravi's room without him calling out, "Honorable father of April. One little moment."

"He's lonely, poor kid," Dad said.

"What does he look like?"

"Normal, I guess. Nice smile. Sorry, April."

"He has to be the guy in the caftan with the gorgeous brown eyes."

"If you know, why ask me?"

"Did you see any photos of his family?"

"Nope. Why?"

"I just wondered if they . . . looked exotic. If his sisters wore saris and rode elephants, you know."

"I'm going to have to remind that young man that this is only friendship, not bride purchase," Dad said, chuckling one night. "Incidentally, there are no photos in his room."

He'd carved me a pumpkin for Halloween and couldn't find space for it on the night table because of Ravi's yellow roses. Fresh roses arrived every Tuesday, a different color every week. Then on Thursday the See's Candy truck made a special stop at our hospital for patients who ordered sweets to keep up their weight, and Ravi put in a standing order. Nancie and I could choose. My favorite flavor was California brittle, hers was English toffee.

"And we've never even met."

"That explains it!" Dad made room for his pumpkin and lit the candle inside.

"Oooh, nice. But can't you tell Dr. Shipman to take me off bed rest and let me go to fluoroscope? It's not like I'm asking to go trick-or-treating."

"The Great Man? Afraid not."

We both laughed. Dr. Shipman was a terror, all right.

"I ask him every week. Just phone once, Dad. Please."

Dr. Shipman finally let me go upstairs to fluoroscope one lovely day in the middle of November. Without warning. I was lying there looking at Mount Tamalpais, clear after a foggy week, when Mary Jane simply marched in and took my woolen robe out of the closet.

"Doctor says you're to come upstairs today," she said in the way she had that always made me feel I'd done something wrong.

"But not in that robe—"

"This robe or stay put. It's cold today."

I shrugged. Okay. It was a pretty enough red Pendleton and I'd feel more—normal in it, not like I was trying to seduce Ravi in Aunt Gretchen's lavender satin. Besides, the windows stayed open here all year and it *was* getting cold. Nancie says it's a wonder we all don't get pneumonia and die. Dr. Shipman says fresh air heals the lungs.

"At least let me go to the bathroom first?" I asked Mary Jane.

"Well, snap it up." I'd been taken off bedpans last

week so she could hardly refuse. Surreptitiously I slipped my makeup bag into a pocket and headed to the bathroom to see what I could do about my face. And my hair! I thought of wearing one of his roses in my hair, but I'd never live it down. Unfortunately, Nancie loved to tease—not to mention Mary Jane. Better not.

Nancie was already in the bathroom, eating bananas. She'd heard from the Mayor of Chinatown that if you ate one banana and half a glass of water just before weighing in, you'd be almost a pound heavier. Only until you went to the bathroom, of course. The trouble was that she was up to four bananas and two glasses of water just to stay at last week's weight.

"Hope my bladder holds out," she said.

"Wear a diaper. Hey, I'm going to fluoroscope!"

"Congratulations!"

Nancie and I both climbed the stairs to the second floor slowly, so we were near the end of the line and I didn't see anyone ahead of us in a caftan. Ravi'd said he was the only guy here who wore one. "Can you see him?" I asked Nancie.

"Not yet."

"Oh, joy. Maybe he can't come today!" I looked in the room across from us and a muscular young man with lively blue eyes waved and crooked his finger for me to come in.

"Hi, how goes it?" I asked.

45

"Don't," Nancie whispered. "This guy plays baseball, too, an outfielder for Oakland. He's having an affair with the night nurse. Too hot for you to handle." Nancie pulled me past the room.

I knew the woman in the next room slightly. Eleanor Warren was an astronomer who'd been here seven years, longer than anyone in the hospital now that Irving had died. Her husband had met someone else and wanted a divorce. Eleanor was willing, but their daughter said she'd never speak to either of them as long as she lived if they got one. So far they hadn't. But she was a stupid girl. My mom and dad both said they were happier after the divorce. And it was easier to be with them one at a time, that was for sure.

I was just about to say hello to Eleanor when I felt a hand on my shoulder and smelled a familiar musky cologne, the scent that clung to the letters Mrs. York brought every morning. I whirled and there he was, smiling broadly. A smile that faded little by little as I continued staring at him.

"Ravi," I said softly. I couldn't stop staring. He was just so . . . foreign. I mean, you could tell instantly he'd been sent to private schools. He had the gentleman look. He was taller than me and small-boned. Very slender, but not skinny or sickly. His gorgeous brown eyes were to drown in, and his smile—well. Even Mary Jane smiled back at Ravi. Lovely olive skin. So why couldn't I tell him I was glad to meet him? I mean, aside from a scrawny mustache, this was really a handsome guy. Worth the wait! So what was wrong?

Maybe it was only that Mike would make two of Ravi, muscle-bound swimmer that he was. Mike had asked me on the postcard in my pocket to write and say I'd go to the prom with him. He hadn't a clue. Should I even answer?

But Ravi's eyes had begun to get that look that dogs get sometimes, when they're being punished and don't know why. I had to get over this and untangle my tongue. "We finally meet. And I can thank you for the flowers and candy and your letters. Dazzling letters." I had to grin at the memory of those letters, and his face lit up.

"You are even more beautiful than I remembered."

"Likewise."

I don't think he quite knew what *likewise* meant, but fortunately Nancie nudged us to move ahead, saying, "Even I have to thank you because April shares her roses and candy."

"As generous as she is lovely. But—you do not like the mustache I am growing for you?"

Then both Nancie and I laughed. "Shave it off at once," I ordered, glad to be able to blame the mustache.

"Mustaches tickle," Nancie added, causing Ravi and me to blush, though it was highly unlikely I'd get a chance to find out.

We had come to the fluoroscope room and I was next. Suddenly I realized that this was the first time the doctors would see my lung since I'd hemorrhaged. Oh, God!

"They will see nothing new," Ravi said quietly. "Do not worry."

For such an understanding heart I would have liked to kiss him, mustache and all. I grasped his hand for an instant and then disappeared into that dark room.

7

THE NEXT MORNING Mrs. York brought me a picture of Ravi along with his usual letter.

"Thanks. I'll look at it later," I said, closing my eyes. Mrs. York was great, but she did love to talk and I had stuff on my mind. In fluoroscope yesterday Dr. Shipman had said my cavity had not grown bigger since the hemorrhage. So I said, "What a relief," the way anyone would. But then Dr. Clark sighed and mumbled something about still having the same problem. The Great Man had shrugged, snapped off the fluoroscope and opened the door, and before I could ask a question, I was back in the hall. I guess they meant that every time I took a breath I opened the cavity. Dr. S. didn't seem to think it mattered, and Dr. Clark did. So long as my lung wasn't damaged by the hemorrhage I was happy.

I reached out for Ravi's letter. The picture fell out and I studied his face without a mustache. A sepia-colored movie-star pose—full face, brown eyes looking straight into my heart. As the days went by I could take his picture from my drawer and tell him—anything. I felt he understood.

I was looking at Ravi's picture the following Sunday morning when Nancie let out a hair-raising scream. "Oh, the dirty son of a bitch, the dirty son of a bitch."

"Nancie, what happened? Tell me," I cried, pulling back the curtain between us to find her shredding the newspaper all over her bed. It was something my mom might do on a very bad day when the paper had stories about Hitler. "Hey, what're you doing?"

Nancie looked up, her eyes frantic, but before she could say anything except "Dino," Mary Jane and Mrs. York came running in. Mary Jane was puffing and red-faced.

"What on earth, Nancie—?" Mary Jane stood at the end of the bed, hands on hips, staring at the shredded newspaper, which, by this time, also covered the floor. "Who do you think is going to clean this up? I'm in the middle of a bed bath."

Mary Jane took the wastepaper basket and started picking up the shredded sports section. Down on all fours she looked as square as a hippopotamus.

"Save Herb Caen. It's in his column," Nancie sobbed.

I scanned Herb Caen in my paper and found the item. "Who's the beautiful blonde that Oaks pitcher Dino Corrado's been squiring around town? Friends say the happy pair are shopping for a diamond ring."

"But Dino was here last night. He brought you

50

candy. This is just some press agent's plant . . ." My voice trailed off as I handed the article to Mary Jane. It was true he hadn't been coming as often lately because they'd been fighting. Or was he out with this blonde?

"Oh, little one, so hard to be young here," Mrs. York said, putting her arms around Nancie and patting her back and crooning. Nancie cried all over Mrs. York's starched white uniform.

"He's not worth the powder to blow him to hell," Mary Jane said, handing back my paper.

"He's weak, but God knows he's the only man I've ever wanted." Nancie sobbed, wiping her tears.

I believed her and maybe the nurses did too, because, for a moment, we were all quiet.

Finally Mrs. York said, "It was that way for me, too." Then she kissed the cross around her neck.

"How can you know he's the only man for you till you've tried others—and with your looks—"

"No! Never, Mary Jane, never! I'll die first."

"Talk to him, tell him," Mrs. York suggested, sinking down on Nancie's chair to rest her swollen feet.

I lay back on my pillows. I could hardly breathe. Nancie's last words echoed in my brain, sending shivers down my spine. This would be such an easy place to die.

Then Mary Jane, meanest nurse in the hospital, let Nancie, who'd just been put on strict bed rest, walk upstairs to the public phone and make several calls. I know there were several because she took every bit of the change all three of us had and didn't come back for an hour. If even Mary Jane spoiled Nancie, how could Dino be two-timing her? I didn't believe it.

When she and the nurses came back, Nancie reported, "He said they broke up last week. It was just that he was missing going out and I've been here three years. But he loves me, worse luck, he says. I don't know."

"He's sorry," Mrs. York said.

"It's hormones," Mary Jane said.

Mike is sure to be taking someone home from the swim meet parties these Saturday nights, I thought. He's always wild to talk and neck later, to unwind.

I reached over and picked up his postcard. "Hey, babe," he wrote. "Save May 17. My senior prom. We'll dance all night. Whoopee. All my love, Mike." Dance all night in six months? Hah! I should show this to Dr. Shipman. Mike had never even come to see me.

That afternoon Mrs. York brought a short note from Ravi. When I read it I felt better. "That Dino will not darken your doorway until the exquisite Nancie misses him so badly she won't dare to be angry with him. Men like him are not unknown, even in my own family." I looked a long while at those two notes and wiped away a few tears. I wasn't going to any senior prom. But wouldn't it be fun to go somewhere with Ravi?

And Ravi was right. Nancie's mother came out the next day with an armload of calla lilies and feet that hurt as badly as Mrs. York's. She and Nancie talked in Italian for a couple of hours. About all I could understand was that they both blamed Dino's mother.

But it was another week, Thanksgiving night, before Dino showed up with a measly half dozen red roses. I wanted to ask what blonde got the other half dozen. But I wasn't speaking to Dino so I couldn't.

"Let's not waste time talking about something that's over," was the nearest Dino came to apologizing.

"So long as she's out of the picture, darling, I couldn't agree more," said Nancie, all peaches and cream. She'd even washed her hair, which was forbidden and caused her temperature to go up.

I'd been gloomy all day, reliving Thanksgiving dinners we used to have with Mom at the Golden Dragon. This year Mom was in her hospital and I was here. She had said if we wrote to each other at two P.M. it would be almost like being together. It wasn't! Dad had gone to the Golden Dragon without me, invited by the owners for a major feast celebrating the end of the war. He didn't get over to see me until after dark.

Dino had already gone and my father was just leaving when a man from a pet store came in carrying a Victorian birdcage tied up with an enormous red velvet bow. Inside, a tiny green-and-yellow parakeet was singing its head off. Well, not exactly singing, but chirping away like a champion.

"Well, that's certainly a sultan's birdcage," Dad said, laughing.

I was reading the card the deliveryman handed me. "It's from Ravi. He says, 'I do not know the proper gift for your so felicitous holiday of gratitude, blessed Thanksgiving, but please to think of our love when you hear my emissary sing.'"

"The gentleman forgot to buy seed, but I brought along a little," said the deliveryman.

Dad sighed. "That's Ravi, too."

"She's the best chirper in the shop," added the deliveryman. "Her wings are clipped so you can let her out. She loves to climb."

"She? I'll call her 'Scheherazade'! And she'll sing of magic lands and a princely lover."

"But I've already spent a thousand and one nights here," groaned Nancie, who'd pulled back her curtain. "Such a cutie, but ten to one the nurses won't let you keep her."

"There's no rule against pets, is there?"

Nancie shrugged. "I've never heard of so much as a goldfish here. And can you see Mary Jane cleaning out a birdcage?"

"Tell them I'll do it," promised Dad, waving as he went out the door.

In another minute or so, far down the hall, eight rooms away, I could hear my father thanking Ravi. He had filled Scheherazade's grain and water dishes before leaving, and the bird ate heartily, clicking at the seed with her beak, scattering sunflower hulls and seed with a vengeance. When she was through I gingerly put my hand inside the cage, palm down, and, miraculously, she climbed on my hand and started to chirp. Oh, Scheherazade!

Hardly daring to breathe, I eased her out of the cage. She climbed out on two fingers and wrapped her claws around my knuckles for balance. We looked at each other. "All right," I said. "Are we friends, then? Would you like to learn to talk?"

Scheherazade inched her way up my arm and it tickled something awful, but I kept still and made what I hoped were soft bird cooing sounds. When she got to my shoulder she perched there and began chirping again.

"Shall I tell you all my secrets?"

I could have sworn she was chirping "Yes, yes, yes."

"Sounds like you're falling for that parakeet," Nancie said, giggling.

"She's prettier than Ravi." But how could I get her back in the cage? As it turned out, after a few minutes Scheherazade made the journey back down my arm and stood on my hand and chirped, as if to say "put me back." So I did, covering the cage with a towel. "We go to bed early here, Scheherazade."

About an hour later the new night nurse for our floor came in for ten P.M. temperatures and medications. Boris, a Russian sailor about forty years old, liked to say he "became nurse to put the pretty girls to bed." He was a big blond bear of a guy who'd jumped ship early in the war when Russia still sided with the Nazis and had gotten political asylum. It was that or Siberia, he told Ravi.

As he picked up the edge of Scheherazade's covering towel and looked into the cage, I saw an enormous smile spread over his face.

"*Ptichka,*" he told the sleeping bird, "after you— never the same, is changed this *tiurma,* this sad hospital, forever!" And then, turning to me, "Present from Ravi, no?"

"Yes."

"That little guy, he knows how to live. Good taste in women, too." Then Boris laughed, disappearing out the door before I could ask just what he meant by that. Boris wouldn't explain anyhow. "No spik English," he'd say.

I was just settling down after that when the door opened again and there stood Ravi himself!

8

"OOOOH," I WHISPERED. Ravi would be in *big* trouble, even with Boris on duty, if he got caught in my room at eleven P.M. There was absolutely no visiting after lights out, especially not by members of the opposite sex, even if you were on exercise, which Ravi wasn't. "You're a lovely guy, but crazy! You'll get us thrown out."

"It is the traditional present for your Thanksgiving, a little singing bird?"

"Well, not exactly, but wonderful. Thank you! Her name's Scheherazade," I whispered.

"Can you believe I am come to make your acquaintance, Scheherazade?" Ravi said. He walked over to us, delicately lifted the towel covering the birdcage and peered in, nearly giving me heart failure.

"Hey, don't get her started chirping or she'll wake Nancie!"

"Not to worry! Sleep in peace, Scheherazade." He

gently let the towel drop back and sat down. Ravi kept nodding as he looked around, reading titles on books, smelling the pink roses he'd sent, picking up a slipper and balancing it on the palm of his hand, then looking out the window at the hummingbird feeder. "Yes, yes, of course. Yes, just as I expected," he kept saying.

Almost three months at opposite ends of one little hall and we'd never seen each other's rooms! It was bizarre, if I let myself think about it. But why tonight? He was looking around as if he'd already visualized my room and now found everything in its proper place. And he kept turning back to me with the sweetest, gentlest smile. Moonlight showed the tenderness in his brown eyes. I could drown in those eyes. He looked like the prince out of a fairy-tale book with his full lips and delicate bone structure, the shock of hair falling over his forehead. Ravi looked chiseled and manly, his high cheekbones mysteriously shadowed. He looked as healthy as Mike these days.

Suddenly, without warning, he pulled the chair toward my bed and, leaning over, kissed me right on the lips. Then he leaned his head against my cheek.

"So beautiful," he said. Did he mean me or the kiss? I agreed, if he meant the kiss. I couldn't bring myself to remind him I was contagious. But he probably was too, so that was okay. It had been months since I'd kissed anyone, and it took me a while to push him away. In fact, his kiss almost made me pass out.

"It's all right. We'll be engaged," Ravi said happily.

"My dad said we could only be friends," I finally managed.

"Oh, well—such very good friends," said Ravi with a wave of his hand as he leaned over me again.

"Shhh, someone in the hall." We froze. Footsteps entered the room next door. "Now, go—quick. Boris'll be here next."

"I say to him I sleepwalk." Ravi grinned and blew me a kiss before he slipped out as quietly as he'd arrived.

What had gotten into him tonight? After three months. After lights out, no less. We'd be lucky if we didn't both get kicked out. At least that's what everyone was saying would happen to the baseball player and the nurse upstairs.

I listened for Boris's outraged voice, but the hall remained quiet. Ravi Bannerjee, master Houdini of the universe, must have made it back to his room. Ravi, whose kisses sparked dreams I'd be ashamed to put down on paper. Maybe I would marry and go to India after all.

The next evening my father came with five pounds of birdseed in a cookie jar. He fed Scheherazade, who chirped away gratefully, and then he shoved the jar under my bed.

"I had a phone call from Dr. Shipman this afternoon," he said.

"Oh?" Fear tore through me like lightning. "What did he want?"

"To warn me about you and Ravi. Seems the parakeet makes him think Ravi has designs on you."

"You told him I hope so?"

"According to him, you're too young to know what you want."

"In India I'd be married." I could feel my cheeks blush scarlet, brighter than the tubercular flush we all had when we got tired. Had Mary Jane found out and told Dr. Shipman about Ravi sneaking in and kissing me last night?

"I told him you cheer each other up and the long hall's as good as a moat. For a clincher, I volunteered to take full care of the bird."

"He's not going to make me give up Scheherazade!"

"Hey, take it easy, April. Dr. Shipman sputtered some about patients wanting dogs next, but in the end he said you could keep the bird. However, if you were his daughter he'd be more particular about the company you keep."

"Yeah, and he'd only let me read *Little House on the Prairie,* too."

"Of course, I could have mentioned Ravi's letter to me about living in harmony and a possible marriage."

"He'd kick us both out."

"I gathered there are days when Dr. Shipman wouldn't mind sending Ravi home to India, but he's fond of you. He says you're no vegetable."

Whatever that meant. Dr. Shipman's compliments usually had a sting, so I didn't ask. Dad grinned and dug into his briefcase, handing me the newspaper he brought every evening. He poured us each tea from his Thermos, passed the box of See's candy, and settled down to the morning paper, reading aloud anything he thought would interest me. I scanned the afternoon paper, also sharing aloud, relieved the doctor didn't know about Ravi's midnight visit.

My father's father and grandfather had both been newspapermen, so naturally we read the papers together, beginning the year I came to live with Dad after the divorce, when Mom left for Carmel to write poetry. Dad used to be a reporter like Grandpa and Great-grandpa but found he liked writing movie scripts better. He's the visual type.

I'd let Scheherazade out of her cage and she perched on my shoulder, reading too.

"April, look." Nancie got a coughing fit trying to tell me something. Finally she got control of her voice. She pulled back her curtain and pointed. "Look. Look. The piano in the courtyard."

Even Dad put down his paper and stood looking out the window, down the hill to the house in the hospital courtyard, where the hospital owner and her handsome husband, who was half her age, lived. Three husky men were carrying a grand piano into the house.

"So they're getting a piano before the holidays," Dad said, without a clue how hard some people here, especially Nancie, were trying to pretend Christmas wasn't on the agenda.

"But, don't you see, that's my piano. I paid for it," Nancie snapped.

"You loaned her the money?"

"Haven't I been paying for that Steinway every month for the last three years? This place costs an arm and a leg. She probably can't play a note—and she's got my piano."

"How do you know it's a Steinway?" asked Dad.

"Nancie plays the piano. She was going to play with an orchestra," I said.

"Used to play. I hate her for having it, hate her, hate her, hate her, hate her! For two cents I'd go down there and play it myself."

"Well—maybe she plays well and she'll serenade you," Dad said, always at a loss when somebody got that hysterical edge to her voice.

"I'd like to take an ax to it," Nancie said.

"Well, don't," Dad said.

We were quiet then, the three of us, watching that piano angled into the front door down the hill as evening shadows deepened and lights flickered on across the hillside facing the hospital. Each of us was thinking of other Christmases. For Nancie and me that piano had suddenly evoked all we'd lost in the world outside. The life she and I might never have again.

"Papa's never come to see me—not once in three years. His mama died of tuberculosis and he says he has to stay well to work and pay my bills," Nancie said quietly.

"At least Dino comes," I said, thinking of Mike.

Nancie's sigh was like an explosion. "Ravi's here," she said.

"Which reminds me, April. Mike called. He said he wrote to you and told you he can't visit because his mother's too afraid for him. He wishes you'd write him back."

"Thanks Dad. Mike's the original Cowardly Lion." I knew Mike was history, but did he have to phone Dad to remind me I was contagious?

And then someone began to play the new grand piano and a vaguely familiar melody drifted softly on the evening air.

"Debussy," said Dad. "Your mother used to play that. By the way, have you heard from her lately?"

I nodded. "She's feeling 'poorly' and doesn't want you to know."

"Aaah. Well. She does the best she can. Someone plays well down there. Nancie, at least you won't have to listen to 'Chopsticks,' " Dad said, neatly easing himself off the subject of Mom. I knew he was paying her hospital bills as well as mine.

"If I could just look in the window and see the darn piano," Nancie said.

9

A FEW DAYS AFTER Thanksgiving the radio started playing "White Christmas," and Boris went up and down the hall singing Christmas carols in Russian.

"Shut up, Boris," Nancie yelled. "Communists aren't supposed to sing Christmas carols."

The prospect of another Christmas in bed spooked her so badly that she asked Dino to bring her earplugs. After my father set up a little Christmas tree on our bureau, she snapped at me.

"April, unplug the lights. They'll keep me awake."

"No, leave them. You're lucky girls. Have the prettiest tree. Enjoy," Boris said, coming in to change water pitchers.

"Really the prettiest? Dad decorated it. Doesn't our room smell like the forest on Mount Tamalpais?"

"So pretty smell like in Russian forest."

"Oh, Lord," said Nancie.

Five minutes later Boris returned carrying two red poinsettia plants as tall as I am. They were trees. The Mayor of Chinatown, our next-door neighbor since Irving died, had sent them. Aunt Gretchen sent an azalea. Mike sent a plush cougar, our high school mascot. Cards and gifts arrived in every mail. Ravi sent a seed wreath for Scheherazade's cage and more roses for me.

"Listen, April. Neither Mike, your mother nor your aunt Gretchen, my father nor anyone at all in Ravi's family have set foot in here. Why? Because they're afraid of us, of the lunger's disease, that's why. So they send us all this merchandise to make themselves feel like they're good people," Nancie said.

But it was beautiful and exciting all the same. It was Christmas and I was happy. "My mother's sick," I said.

"So much Christmas junk I can't even get in with your breakfast trays," Mary Jane grumbled, plunking down my tray along with a large manila envelope from my swim coach.

I ignored her and tore it open. A scrapbook of swim meet newspaper clippings! Tears again. Stop it, I commanded myself as I flipped through and noticed pictures of Mike coming in first. He was really doing well. He must be heading for a championship!

"Hey, Nancie, want to see a picture of my old boyfriend?"

"Maybe I'll run away instead," Nancie said. "Just

kidding. Mary Jane, would you be an angel and bring it so April doesn't hemorrhage on the picture?"

"Ravi's my guy."

"Poor soul," said Mary Jane, taking the envelope.

Then, two weeks before Christmas, Ravi walked into our room one day after naps.

"You're here in plain daylight?" I clapped my hand over my mouth.

"I have the exercise. Twenty minutes a day. I am— what you call—legal."

"Then why aren't you outside walking?" Nancie asked.

"I walk here. Congratulate me!"

"No, it's stupid coming here. I'd be outside looking in the window at that grand piano. Then I'd walk all around the grounds. I've always wanted to see where they keep the caskets—and the crematory."

"The what?" I screamed.

"Where they burn corpses."

"Here?" I asked.

"Between us and the main hospital. Can't see it from here, but it's there, somewhere."

"How do you know?"

"Ask Mrs. York. Everyone knows."

"You're kidding, right?" But I could feel the goose pimples starting. Creepy.

"A pyre. Setting free the spirit," Ravi said.

"Ravi, you go look and tell us if there is a pyre—crematorium," I said.

"I'm sorry I told you."

"Why, Princess Nancie?" Ravi asked.

Nancie had tears in her eyes. "Because—it was the first place I was going when I got on exercise. Three years I've been thinking of thumbing my nose at that darn crematory."

"Then," Ravi said quietly, "we will all go."

Nancie and I stared.

"Are you out of your mind? We can't even walk down the hall—except on Monday," I said. Except on Monday for fluoroscope. A little walk around the grounds couldn't be worse for us than standing around upstairs for hours. I pursed my lips.

Suddenly Nancie laughed, her great full-out laugh that I hadn't heard since Herb Caen wrote about Dino's blonde. "How?" she asked.

"We'd get caught before we got out the door," I said.

"Not on Thursday." Ravi dropped his voice to a whisper.

"Thursday? How about Monday after—?"

"Too crazy with Dr. Shipman popping up everywhere, April. Ravi, go on. I know Mary Jane leaves at two on Thursdays for her class. But Mrs. York stays until Boris comes at three. And the whole world knows April and I are not on exercise."

"With naptime until two-thirty, Mrs. York is resting her poor crippled feet. Is true, no?"

"Yeeeah. Count me in." Nancie's smile lit up the room. I couldn't believe this was happening, but when Ravi looked at me, I nodded too.

"Our first date," he said, and, looking at his watch, made for the door. "A date we have," he repeated, and started down the hall to his room. His twenty minutes' exercise was over.

The next three days we said nothing more but thought of little else. Each day, when he left our room after exercise, Ravi would say, "Remember, a date we have."

"Yeeeah," Nancie would answer, laughing softly.

I would gulp and say nothing. I was scared of getting caught. Scared of making myself sicker. Dad was paying a lot to keep me here so I could get well.

Meanwhile, Ravi and I trained Scheherazade, whose wings were clipped, to walk down the hall and visit Ravi and then bring a message back to me.

"Nothing but a nuisance, and God only knows how many diseases the stupid bird's carrying," Mary Jane said.

"Dr. Shipman said I could have her. He says she'll sing me well."

"Hah!"

I shrugged and turned my back, scrunching into the pillow to get comfortable. "I'm only afraid you might step on Scheherazade."

"Good idea," said Mary Jane, flouncing out of our room.

Thursday morning it rained. I heard the rain on the roof and Nancie crying before I even opened my eyes.

"It'll stop by ten o'clock," I said, though I saw the rain as a sign of deliverance. I didn't really think our going off the reservation, as Nancie called it, would hurt us. But Dr. Shipman would say it'd kill us and he did make you wonder.

By ten A.M. we had a rainbow and by eleven the sky was blue.

"Hey, kid, you got it right," Nancie said happily.

"I cannot get my legs comfortable in this miserable bed any way at all this morning," I said.

"Boy, have we got the cure for that!"

A little before two we saw Mary Jane marching down the path, and one minute later Ravi was in our room with two bathrobes I'd never seen before in my life and two wool caps.

"Disguises for my princesses." He laughed, holding up a plaid flannel robe for me and a flowered quilted robe for Nancie. "And all your hair hide under the caps."

We didn't stop to ask where he'd gotten the robes. We quickly put them on and tiptoed out past the empty office and through the back door.

Outside! I stood in a patch of sunlight for the first

time in three months. Ravi and I looked at each other and, as if he were magnetized, I moved into his open arms.

"Our first date," he murmured, kissing me.

"Hey, come on," Nancie urged.

She was halfway down the path. We caught up and walked quietly, his arm around my waist. Personally, I was overwhelmed by sunlight, by the smells of lavender and narcissus, by birds I could almost touch, by Ravi.

"We go left here," Nancie whispered.

"The piano," Ravi explained.

I wasn't afraid anymore because it didn't seem real to be walking in front of the owner's garden cottage.

"Damn it to hell," Nancie groaned.

I nodded. Venetian blinds closed off every window! An orange cat meowed and rubbed against the house but, seeing us, disappeared around the corner.

"Perhaps, you ring the doorbell and ask to play the so beautiful piano," Ravi said, and laid his hand on Nancie's shoulder briefly.

"Thanks for nothing. Okay, I think we go down and to the right—"

It was a relief to be out of sight of the sanitarium windows. No sense in begging patients to look out and wonder who Ravi was walking with. Suddenly, set a fair distance from other structures, we saw a dreary-looking square cement building. It had to be the crematory.

Amazingly enough, the door was open, and we ventured inside. It was bad enough outside, but the inside was really depressing. The walls, the floor, and a cement bench were all painted hospital white. In the center was an oven-type apparatus, about seven feet long and narrow.

"Just the size for a body," Nancie whispered.

"In my country, we release the spirit of the dead in a big fire by the holy waters. Out in the open, before God and everyone," Ravi said, going over and pulling open the oven door. It creaked eerily.

"Just like an oven," I said in a shaky voice.

"That's because it *is* an oven," Nancie said. "Who's gonna try it?"

"I will," Ravi said. I thought it was gallant of him to volunteer.

"No, I will," Nancie said in such a strange voice that Ravi and I were stunned for a moment. We stepped aside.

But as she bent to look inside, her face went so dead white that Ravi took her arm, saying, "Not you, Nancie, you'll get a coughing spell."

I stepped in front of Nancie. "Me, then. I want to feel what it's like to be dead." Where I got the courage I'll never know, but I crawled in and stretched out on my back. The slab was cold and the ceiling low. It felt like a tomb. I started shaking. I was terrified.

Suddenly Nancie made a strange whinnying noise,

reached over and closed the door with a clunk. I was alone in the dark. Stone cold in my grave. I couldn't turn over or get out. Ever.

"No," Ravi snapped. He pulled the door open.

"I wanted her to see what death was like too," Nancie said.

I scooted out, pushing forward with my feet, and ran to the door and out of that house of death as fast as my trembling legs could take me. Not until I was halfway up the path did I stop to catch my breath. My heart was pounding. I turned to see if the others were following and waited, hugging myself to quiet my shivering.

"I don't know what got into me. It was a bad joke— sorry," Nancie said, gasping for breath.

"I guess you were only playing." What if Ravi hadn't been there?

"And only you, my brave one, saw into the future," Ravi said with what sounded like envy.

"Not my future! Now's the scary part. Getting back in."

"Back to jail." Nancie said what we all thought, and we were somber as we climbed back up the incline to the sanitarium.

There was one terrible moment. Just as Ravi opened the door and stepped in, Mrs. York came out into the hall from a room halfway down. Ravi slammed the door on me and Nancie, called loudly to the nurse and walked her on down to his room. I could hear him telling her he'd wanted to see the grand piano but the venetian blinds were closed. "So unfriendly, never all this shutting up in India."

Nancie opened the door stealthily and we crept around the office and back into our room, stuffed the borrowed robes in our spare drawer, and climbed into our beds.

I hadn't felt all that tired when we were outside, but now I was totally exhausted, as grateful to be in bed as I had been the awful first day I came. All I wanted was to lie in bed and admire the Christmas tree. Safe. Safe. Safe. I lay there shivering, wondering how Nancie, sicker than I, must feel. But she was silent and it was an unspoken rule here that you never asked if someone felt sick.

I was almost asleep when Nancie, in a soft voice, said, "I'd forgotten how much fun it is—outside. Totally, totally worth it."

"Worth what?" I asked drowsily.

Nancie sighed but didn't answer.

10

THE NEXT MORNING I was back to TB normal, which is weak and running a temperature but feeling okay if I didn't push it. Nancie, however, was coughing a lot, and she looked white as a ghost. I saw Mary Jane give her a sharp look and take her pulse when she brought in breakfast. You'll never guess where we've been, Mary Jane, I thought. Never in a million years! But maybe yesterday was too much for Nancie, even if I was the one locked in when she shut the oven door. Closed the door, she said, so I'd know how it felt to be dying too, the way she did. Was she jealous because I hoped to get well and she'd given up? That was crazy. That was too scary! She was having a low day, that's all.

The following Monday Nancie had to eat six bananas and drink three glasses of water before we went up to fluoroscope. And that just kept her weight even. She looked awfully skinny. It must have taken her half an hour to get the bananas down, and it made me gag just watching her. Thank God I never started that.

The Mayor of Chinatown had quit the banana routine two weeks before. He'd told Dr. Shipman what he had been doing and we'd heard the doctor yelling that if he pulled one more stunt like that he'd have to leave the hospital. If Dr. Shipman would yell at a dignified old man of seventy, what would he do to her? So Nancie didn't dare say a word. Nor did the other three patients on our floor who had Boris buying them bananas.

"I feel like I'm getting the flu," she said after she'd eaten all the bananas.

"Maybe you shouldn't go to fluoroscope this morning."

"What? After choking down those damn torpedoes? And miss my only chance all week to talk to anyone but you and the nurses? I'd die first."

So we set off, Nancie quite weak and neither of us too steady on our feet. As usual, we were toward the end of the line, and as usual, Ravi was waiting for us at the top of the stairs. To stay out of trouble with Dr. Shipman, Ravi and I didn't even hold hands. We just stayed close together.

Since this was the week before Christmas, we wanted to take what Ravi called the grand tour. Most rooms had some decoration for the holidays. Only people on exercise could normally visit other patients, so the rest of us snatched at chances to be with each other.

The baseball player's door was closed. Mrs. York had said he was too too sick, and the silence behind that closed door was ominous.

"Damned if you do and damned if you don't. Poor guy," Nancie said.

"The doctor yelled at him that he might as well take an ax to his lung as have a love affair. All the way down the hall we heard them," a man in front of us whispered.

The next room belonged to Eleanor, the astronomer whose husband was going ahead with the divorce after she'd been here seven years. The whole hospital knew their daughter had phoned and said it was "the last time you'll ever hear my voice, Mother." Eleanor's back was to us, and she didn't turn when Ravi called her name. I hated her daughter passionately.

"Perhaps, some patients do not decorate because they come, like me, from some far land without your so lovely Christmas," said Ravi.

"Hah! Mrs. York said you ordered a decorated tree from a florist, so don't give me that far land baloney," said Nancie.

"I'm coming down to see it, too, regardless."

"Ah, your presence will be the finest gift of all, my April."

"Well, you're sure the Prince of Blarney today, Ravi." Nancie laughed.

It was good to hear her laugh. We passed three rooms with poinsettia plants and lights strung around the walls. One had a wall of Christmas cards. One had a tiny tree. Then we passed a room with an old man looking at an antique silver menorah set on the dresser so that the mirror reflected flickering Hanukkah candles on the walls.

"Ooooh, lovely! So peaceful!"

"Sir, why do you light the candles in the morning?" asked Ravi.

"For good luck in the fluoroscope. You know our customs, then?" The old man propped himself on one elbow and smiled.

"My tutor would let me light a candle on Friday evening."

"I didn't know you had a tutor, Ravi. Did he teach your sisters, too?"

"My beautiful April, our days together here enthrall me so I do not choose to remember my past. Our tutor came every morning by rickshaw and taught us the history of our world. When he left the math professor came on his bicycle. Then a lady taught my sisters how to be ladies while I walked with the cobra trainer to the English school in the next compound. The cobras were dangerously restless in their sack."

"The cobra trainer?" But we were getting near the fluoroscope room, and that heavy metal door opening and closing was working its usual twisting in my gut. We all fell silent.

Nancie groaned.

"Uh-oh," I said, knowing the struggle she must be

having to keep from running to the bathroom after three glasses of water.

"Both ends," she said.

"Hang on, only one inside and then you take my turn."

Nancie nodded. "Thanks, Ravi."

The door yawned open and the Mayor of Chinatown came out looking serious, not seeing us as he passed. Nancie crossed herself. We watched her walk slowly into the fluoroscope room, the door clanging shut behind her.

"She has the tragic face," Ravi said.

"Nancie's been sicker ever since we—you know, Thursday," I said in a low voice.

Ravi's eyes opened wide and he nodded.

"Oh, Lord—nurse, nurse." Dr. Clark's voice rang out of the fluoroscope room.

Then the door swung open and Dr. Shipman rushed out, carrying Nancie in his arms. They brushed past us, his face a mask. Nancie was crying. There were banana pieces soaked all down the front of her new maroon velvet robe.

"Nurse, clean up this mess," Dr. Clark ordered as he hurried after Nancie and Dr. Shipman.

"Nancie, it's all right," I called after them, but no one answered.

I wanted to follow but didn't have the nerve. So I just stood there. "This was our fault for sneaking out

Thursday. Our fault," I whispered as I slumped down to sit on the floor.

"No, Nancie has been getting worse these last months, very sick, and we try to cheer her with our outing. Nothing wrong, April. A tubercular never stands when he can sit, so I will join you," Ravi added, quoting Dr. Shipman's rule. So he sat. He put his hand over mine, but I gently removed it. We had enough trouble. And, somehow, we were the only ones left to fluoroscope.

"The entire world has forgotten us," Ravi said finally.

"Dad says keeping us up Monday morning and then flat on our backs the rest of the week is the most ridiculous treatment he's ever heard of in his entire life." However, he didn't say this to Dr. Shipman because the hospital had the highest cure rate in California and people came from all over the world to take the cure here. We all felt threatened by the long waiting list.

"A nightingale in the talons of the eagle," said Ravi.

I burst into tears. Dr. Shipman couldn't help knowing about the bananas and maybe the trip to the crematory by this time. Nancie'd been in trouble before. He'd send her home and she'd die. "I have to go down there and see what's going on."

"I offer myself," said Ravi.

But at this moment Dr. Clark and Mary Jane came back.

"All right. Let's get this show on the road," Dr. Clark said. And they ran us through the fluoroscope and weighing in about two minutes. Even if we'd developed new cavities they wouldn't have noticed.

"Blessings be on you and the beauteous Nancie," Ravi said gently as we reached my door.

I nodded, blew him a kiss, and went in. The curtains were drawn around Nancie's bed, but I pulled one back.

"Nancie, are you okay? I've been so worried." I gasped as I saw that Dr. Shipman was still sitting on her bed. Nancie had red, puffy eyes, but she didn't look devastated, only serious. "I'm sorry."

"It's all right, April. Nancie and I were talking about getting well, and there's no reason you shouldn't hear the story of my own tuberculosis, too. As long as you keep my secret. All right? Hop up into bed first, honey."

Then Dr. Shipman smiled that lovely smile of his that made you forget what a beast he could be.

"Well, ladies, I first contracted tuberculosis when I was a young doctor, just finishing my residency. I was luckier than you, Nancie, and healed in a few months. But two years later I was flat on my back again, and this time I had a cavity. To make a long story short, I came down with TB again five times. I don't blame you for gasping. I was one impetuous young fellow. Stupid as they come."

"But you look so—healthy," Nancie said.

That was just what I was thinking. But this was between Nancie and him so I kept quiet. Besides, I was in shock. Five times he'd recovered and then broken down with tuberculosis again. Dr. Shipman!

"I've been healthy for over twenty years now, Nancie, because I had a lobectomy. I'd have been a goner without it. Look at me. Fit as a fiddle." He slid off her bed and stood there with his arms outstretched.

"You had a lobectomy?"

Lobectomy! The most dreaded word in our hospital vocabulary. Last-chance surgery. He only did lobectomies, sawing through ribs to remove the infected lobe of the lung, when he thought a patient wouldn't get well otherwise. The death rate was over twenty percent, and recovery was horrendously painful. Worst of all, you were left with a scar shaped like a sickle down one side of your back. Forever. Most people hunched over after a lobectomy. However, Dr. Shipman stood straight as a general.

"Think about it, Nancie," he said, patting her hand and standing up.

"Oh, no." I bit my lip to make myself shut up.

"It's only Dino, Doctor, otherwise I would."

"It's only your life, my darling girl," said the doctor from the door. "You tell her, April."

Neither Nancie nor I said anything for a while after he left. I was trembling.

"So he wants you to have it." I said the words out loud after it seemed as if we'd been thinking them so long they filled the room. Patients always referred to lobectomy as "it" because this was the last chance.

"He's wanted me to have the surgery for a year, but I won't."

A year! Then it wasn't because we went to the crematory. Relief flooded over me. "Did you know Dr. S. had it? He looks good."

Nancie shook her head. "I didn't know until today. He tried bananas to gain weight too. But he made me promise not to tell."

I grinned and crossed my heart. "Maybe Dino would rather have you home. Maybe he wouldn't mind a scar."

"Damaged goods," Nancie said, and turned her back to me.

"Ask him."

But Nancie pretended not to hear. It was something she did lately, something Mom used to do when she was feeling down. So it made me feel doubly lonely. But who could blame her now? Imagine Dr. S. getting TB again five times. Each time he was back in the hospital knowing he might never come out? And then having that surgery?

"Scheherazade, when we get out of here, we're never coming back, are we—are we?" Nancie was welcome to listen. "And I'd do anything to get out, too."

The parakeet chirped companionably, but even so, I had to reach for Kleenex and wipe away tears.

11

RAVI AND I didn't exactly break up Christmas day, but we came close. What happened was that I'd asked my father to buy Ravi two of my favorite books in the world. Only he'd already read *A Room with a View* and thought *Anna Karenina* "more for the ladies. Could they be exchanged?" Ravi gave me the scarf he'd been knitting under his covers for months. He had dropped more stitches than he'd picked up. And it was a powerful orange, a color that makes my skin look blotchy.

"I couldn't wear that scarf to a rummage sale," I told Dad after Ravi left.

"You made that clear, honey."

"Hey, after all the wonderful presents he's given me—I thought—for Christmas—but Mrs. York had to go and teach him to knit."

"All those lonely hours knitting, he was probably thinking how delighted you'd be. Ravi is by himself here."

"Whose side are you on, Dad?"

"I'm just grateful he didn't try buying you a ring!"

We both laughed.

"A diamond ring! Imagine the look on Mary Jane's face! Or Dr. Shipman's! Actually, I kind of hoped he'd give me a ring—not an engagement ring, just something to stir this place up a little."

"What do you suppose Ravi hoped you might give him?"

"Oh, stop it! If only someone from his maharajah family'd come, I wouldn't have to feel so guilty. But they've deserted him. And now I guess I have."

"That's more like the Christmas spirit," Dad said.

I began to feel worse and worse. All the rest of us were celebrating the holidays with someone. Ravi was probably the only patient on the floor without any company today.

That night, after all the visitors had left and Boris had come through turning off lights and unplugging the Christmas trees, the hospital was painfully silent. Only Boris's footsteps and the ghosts of visitors past echoed after nine-thirty. Footsteps, coughing, groans. "Lordie puss, what a life," my mother said of hospitals. I sat up in bed and looked out. Overhead the sky was alive with stars and a full moon.

All over the surrounding hills, lighted houses clustered like fireflies. Christmas trees shimmered, and healthy families celebrated with their men, newly home from the war after four long years.

And then, suddenly, our door swung open and there stood Ravi in his turquoise cashmere caftan, his grin a little tentative. I pointed toward Nancie's curtained bed because I wasn't sure she was asleep yet. Ravi nodded and came directly to my bed and kissed me, long and hard.

"Merry Christmas, Ravi," I whispered.

"I am at home now," he replied, kissing me again.

"I'm glad."

"Love is our gift for each other. As with the first Christmas, no?"

"Hmm. In that caftan you even look like one of the wise men." Dad was right. I'd hurt Ravi. "All those hours knitting. Were you really thinking of me?"

His smile said it all. And his kiss. Kissing Ravi was passionate but also comfortable, and I felt like going on and on.

Which is why neither of us heard Boris come in. I looked up to find him standing there at the foot of my bed. We stared at each other. I bit my lip to keep from screaming and nudged Ravi.

"You are scaring my April," Ravi whispered sternly, standing up and facing Boris.

"Boris, it is Christmas," I said.

"Enough is enough," Boris muttered.

My terror ebbed a little, just enough to smell a rat. Even on Christmas Boris shouldn't take such an unspeakable breach of rules this calmly. Not even Boris, the most easygoing nurse in the hospital. What I realized suddenly was that Ravi only visited on nights when Boris was on duty.

"I must keep my job to stay in this so beeyootiful country, Ravi. The doctor signed papers for me. And I cannot go home to Russia," he said, drawing a finger across his throat like a sword to show what would happen if he did.

"Ah, I have no wish to make you trouble. I go."

"You say fifteen minutes once a week. Suppose she tell," Boris added, pointing to Nancie's curtained bed. His voice was reproachful. I remembered it was Boris who bought Nancie's bananas. And now Ravi was bribing him. He sure took chances for a man afraid of being deported.

"She's asleep. Shhh—"

"Who can sleep with you guys making out six feet away?" Nancie's light snapped on and she pulled back her curtain. "Merry Christmas, guys."

"See?" Boris's voice was heavy with reproach.

"Boris, forget it. I never tell anyone anything."

"She doesn't." I stared at Nancie under her bed light. We were all staring at her. The sharp chin and intense sunken eyes gave her face a faintly sinister look, as if the weight loss had suddenly changed her from Snow White into the wicked stepmother.

"Turn off your light and we will tell you a big secret," Ravi ordered quickly. "Boris and I, we are thinking about how to welcome the New Year, such a happy time in both our countries. Night and day everyone is lighting firecrackers and celebrating the good omens for the coming year. Especially this year, when the terrible war has ended."

"So much champagne," Boris added.

"Champagne," Nancie echoed wistfully.

"We thought a little party among friends sharing a quiet moment of happiness in this cold hospital," Ravi whispered.

"A party? What happens if they catch us?"

"Who cares?" asked Nancie. With her deep throaty laugh and her moonlit smile, this was Nancie the beautiful again.

"But Boris, can't you be deported?" I asked. "And the rest of us could be thrown out of the hospital. Mary Jane keeps showing us that long list of tuberculars waiting to get in." I figured we'd about used up our luck by exploring the crematory without getting caught.

"And Boris can't go back to Russia," Ravi added sadly.

"One day a year, Boris must live! Friends must celebrate the coming of peace to make it stay," said Boris, pounding his chest.

"How true! And we must welcome the year—or good luck will not follow," Ravi said, happy again. "I will ask to take my exercise after dinner—a privilege for the New Year, which the doctor knows is big holiday in India."

"Boris, will you be okay?" I insisted.

"Not to worry. I say to the other nurses, never mind, I will work. And they are so grateful because they have parties. So you ladies stay safe in bed and we visit and bring the champagne. The upstairs night nurse never comes down. No problem."

The sound of the word *champagne* popped into the air like a celebration. I'd never had any, but I didn't say so. I didn't want them remembering I was underage.

"Let's do it," Nancie said, and so it was decided.

It was pouring on New Year's Eve. Torrents of water battered the earth, running down our hillside in instant rivers. Good. Other patients wouldn't hear our party. However, to be safe, we'd also invited the Mayor of Chinatown, whose room was the only one adjoining ours, the office being on the other side. He was, as Ravi said, grandfather to us all. Or, as Boris said, one old man still young.

Both Dino and my father were at New Year's Eve parties. This had Nancie half out of her mind but made it possible to store iced champagne and a snack tray in our bathroom shower. The very sight of crystal wine glasses put us in a party mood.

"New Year's Eve. Champagne!" Nancie laughed, watching Boris pour the wine after night rounds. We'd gathered around her bed, since she was the weakest. The Mayor, Mr. Wu, had ordered gardenias for every woman on our floor, and we pinned ours in our hair and admired their waxy glow in the candlelight. I wore my lavender satin negligee and Nancie wore filmy black lace from her hope chest.

"Gardenias perfume the New Year night in my garden in India. An avenue of bushes and hundreds of so fragrant blossoms on each bush," Ravi said, inhaling my gardenia.

Tonight Ravi looked like the Indian prince he was, in tight leggings and a long orange silk tunic jacket embroidered in gold. I'd never seen him dressed like this before and couldn't stop staring. My stomach felt queasy. He looked foreign and official, like someone in the movies. And it reminded me that India, so very far away, was Ravi's world, not mine. In his caftans he always looked exotic, an outsider here. But seeing him in uniform, I realized I was the outsider in his world. I shivered with loneliness in a circle of friends.

"And do your sisters wear gardenias in their hair tonight?" Nancie asked. Mrs. York had borrowed a picture from his night table drawer and shown us the two stunning young women in saris.

"Ah, but not so exquisitely as you."

"And soon you'll be returning?" asked Mr. Wu.

"Returning?" Ravi and I asked at the same time.

"Well, you have half an hour exercise. Soon you'll have an hour. Don't you think about going home?"

Nancie reached for her glass and took a long sip, though we hadn't toasted yet.

Ravi shook his head. "No, I must be strong first."

"I fall in love when you smile, Nancie," said Boris, wearing a Russian fur hat and his white uniform. He raised his glass and smiled into her eyes.

"To our homelands—China, Russia, India, and America. Dey do dna." Boris raised his glass and drank the champagne.

We all raised our glasses then and Ravi proposed another toast. "To our health and to peace," he said.

"To health and peace," we each repeated, and drank as if the bubbly elixir might work its magic cure then and there.

"To absent friends," Nancie added, lifting her glass. We all knew she meant Dino, who had come earlier but only stayed half an hour. But I was silently toasting Mike, whose desertion was merely a wish to survive. The Christmas card he'd sent with the stuffed cougar assumed I'd be ready to dance until dawn in time for his senior prom in May. I hadn't sent him anything. No hard feelings? Well, less with my first champagne, wonderful bubbly champagne.

"No, sir, Mr. Wu, my father and I have no impatience for my return." Ravi spoke into the silence following Nancie's toast. "I am to become strong like a tiger." Ravi reached out and took my hand.

I smiled. I was feeling a little dizzy.

"Ah, to be young and have years to spare. I say to doctor every week, send me home, send me home so I may christen my first great-grandson. He laughs and congratulates me and goes away. He has no children and no understanding."

"Boy, you have some nerve, Mr. Wu," Nancie said. "My dog, Ginger, died last week, and I wanted so much to bury her, but I knew better than to ask."

"Nancie! The collie on your wall? What happened?" I was hurt. Why hadn't she told me?

"Old age. We got her when I was five."

"Would you like to see his picture, my great-grandson?" asked the Mayor, handing around an enlarged photo of a plump, smiling Chinese boy about two months old.

We toasted him, too. Then we toasted the baseball player upstairs who had become so dangerously ill.

We were quiet, thinking of the happy young man who waved so eagerly on Mondays and the pretty blond nurse, who, according to rumor, loved him. I had heard him coughing the way Irving did before he died.

"If he dies, will they take him to the crematory?"

"Nancie, shut up." My hands trembled, remembering.

Ravi looked at Nancie and then leaned down and kissed her lightly on the cheek. "He can choose how he wishes to be buried. We all can, Nancie."

Nancie nodded. "Good."

"Enough. No one dies, not on Boris's shift. In Russia I had big family, biiiig family," Boris said, stretching his arms wide as if hugging his relatives. "How many have lived to see the war end, I ask myself? My mother, father, brothers, cousins? Are they tonight at our country dacha toasting absent Boris? Ah, well, a happy New Year to my family!" Boris, the vagabond Russian, had tears in his eyes as he lifted his glass.

"You will go home now the war is over?" Mr. Wu asked.

"No, Mr. Wu, I can never go home."

We lifted glasses to Boris's family. And then, of course, we all had families to toast. Boris refilled our glasses. I wanted to ask why he could never go home to Russia, but my tongue suddenly didn't work right. I cuddled in Ravi's arms, happy and a bit dizzy.

"What?" I asked when Boris toasted again.

"To Mary Jane," he said, raising his glass, a silly grin on his face. "We have what you call here—a date."

"Oh, no—you'll tell on us—"

"No, Nancie, as you say it to me, I tell never anything to anyone. We are the friends, no? Mary Jane is only a date."

So we drank to Mary Jane, though I kept my fingers crossed on that one.

Then we started passing around snapshots, and I saw Ravi's parents and his brother for the first time. His brother looked like a movie star, and his two sisters had lovely dark eyes and an air of silken mystery. As Mrs. York had said before, who could imagine them doing dishes? The elder sister's marriage had been arranged and would take place next month. She was sixteen. My age! The maharajah looked like the handsome movie-star son, except taller, and he had a shock of white hair. Ravi's mother looked straight into the camera, staring down any girl who would encroach on her family. "She doesn't like me," I whispered before I could stop myself.

Ravi looked shocked and I started to explain, but then I saw his face. He knew it was true. She wouldn't like me.

"No matter," said Ravi after what seemed like a long time. "One day with their own eyes they see you with love."

Nancie pointed to her engagement picture. "To Dino and me. I'll give that mama of his grandchildren yet!"

We all clicked glasses, but dizzy as I was, that toast plus seeing Ravi's mother and father for the first time made me feel a little sick. Still, I didn't refuse when Boris filled our glasses one last time, taking only the last couple of drops for himself.

Mr. Wu began to giggle.

Nancie laughed, and I tried, but it came out like a croak.

Boris looked at me sharply. "April, you are red like a New Year's lantern. Too much champagne. Lie back."

Was I drunk? I remember Ravi calling my name, and then the next thing I knew it was morning. I was in bed, still wearing my aunt's negligee, with a wilted gardenia in my hair. I barely had time to change before Mary Jane brought the breakfast trays. I could only hope Boris and Ravi had gotten rid of the champagne bottles and glasses.

"Nancie," I called after Mary Jane left. "What happened to me?"

"Lordie, what a head," she groaned. "Don't ask."

"Did Boris really say he has a date with Mary Jane?"

"Don't ask."

"Did I do—anything terrible?"

"Wouldn't you like to know, April? Beg, come on."

12

"HAPPY NEW YEAR." Mrs. York's wide grin as she delivered Ravi's morning letter made me uneasy. Surely he wouldn't tell Mrs. York about last night? Maybe Mary Jane was already on the phone to Dr. Shipman.

"Last night was an adventure out of the *Arabian Nights,* filled with delights beyond dreaming," Ravi's letter began. Since I'd passed out, I could only suspect he was laying it on pretty thick. I set the letter down and watched Mrs. York, who was assembling basin, water and towels for my bed bath. She touched the cross around her neck for good luck.

"Were you at a party last night?" I asked tentatively.

"Ah, my party days are over, little one. But if you could have been to my engagement party, that was a night! A New Year's Eve to remember!" She'd been as young as me then, this old nurse walking around on feet crippled from torture in a prison camp, who prayed every day for me to get well.

Mrs. York soaped me down, rolled and scrubbed, rinsed and dried and massaged me with alcohol, all the time talking about her engagement party. Her soft, happy brown eyes showed she was enjoying her satin gown and dancing with her sweetheart all over again, making me see her beautiful and in love. She must not know about last night. She'd have said something. She always did.

"Mrs. York, now that the war's over, are you going back to the Philippine Islands?" Was she deserting me, was what I meant.

"Someday. Someday, I visit."

"Boris can't go home but you can?" I asked, drawing my finger across my throat.

She sighed and nodded, then patted my arm and collected the basin and towels.

"For Boris and me this war is never ending," she said, and walked out of the room.

"She's thinking about her husband getting killed," Nancie said.

"Oh."

After Mrs. York left I must have dozed off again because the next thing I heard were angry voices. Nancie had company. Dino. Sounded like she was asking him about last night's party. Who had he gone with? Had he bought the blonde a ring yet?

"If not, you can always give her this one."

"Don't say things you don't mean, Nancie." There was a threat in Dino's voice.

"Ah, Dino, what's to become of us?"

"I'm getting so I can't remember your kiss," he replied with a sigh.

"And your mother wants grandchildren!"

"I'll be thirty in a few months. Thirty, Nancie, thirty! And what's to show for it? I'll never make the majors now. My youth's gone here in this room instead."

Oh, brother! Blaming Nancie because he didn't make the majors. Was it her fault batters could hit his pitches?

"Is it my fault I'm here?" Nancie asked, and I could hear the bitterness in her voice.

"I'm sorry for you, but is it my fault I'm normal?"

"Normal?"

"Healthy. You know what I'm saying, Nancie."

"And?"

"I wish—ah, Nancie, don't make this harder—"

"Don't make what harder?"

Neither said anything more for a long time. Finally Nancie let out a sigh like nothing I'd ever heard before. Despair. "Spit it out, Dino."

"Yeah. Baby, don't look like that. You're scary."

"Are you still waiting for me?" Nancie asked.

Dino groaned then, a sound so sad I could almost feel sorry for him if I didn't hate him. This was no normal fight, no letting off steam and making up next week.

"I've been trying to tell you for months, months, and now—"

"What? Dino, what, my love?"

There was another groan. "Nancie—I'm going to be a father. I never meant to. I love you. I was lonely and you fight with me and it happened, that's all."

"And you've married her?" Her voice dropped, as if they were conspirators.

"Last month but—"

Nancie groaned then, a groan I'll never forget. Never!

And then I could hear them crying—both of them—whispering, sobbing.

Finally Dino cried out, "Nancie I love you, only you, only you forever."

"I've always loved you, and you gave her our baby."

"How can I live without you?" Dino asked.

"Well, you've killed me," Nancie said, her voice low.

It must have been then that she ripped off his ring and threw it out the window, down the hillside of poison oak and blackberry brambles that separated us from the hospital owner's house below.

"Why throw away your ring? Did you think I was going to take the damn ring back? What do you think I am?" And Dino's voice trembled.

"If you want it, go find it."

"Never!"

"Not you, Dino. That mother of yours. She'll come asking for it and I'll just point. She'll hunt for it, too.

Wait and see." And Nancie laughed then. "I want to see her down on her hands and knees, crawling in the poison oak, after what she's done to us."

Dino stalked out after that. His marriage was in the papers the next day. The news had leaked and he knew it and that's why he had to come and tell Nancie.

Otherwise, as Mary Jane said the next day when we showed her the article, Dino would still be coming to woo Nancie when he had three brats. She knew two-timers, she said before she left.

But then Ravi, visiting on the forty minutes' exercise he now had, spoke up. "The reporter did wrong. Our so beautiful Nancie no longer has the visits of her Dino. Dino has the unhappy heart and the bad anger for this other woman and the unborn child. Bad karma for all," he said, shaking his head and looking mournfully over at the other bed, where Nancie lay like a mummy, her eyes closed.

Nancie's eyes flew open at that, and I thought Ravi was going to get the tongue-lashing of his life. I held my breath. But Nancie lay there, not saying anything, staring at Ravi. Finally she sighed, pursing her lips, letting out these little *tut-tut* sounds of hers.

"Takes one to know one," was all she said. Then she closed her eyes again and wouldn't open them, even when Mary Jane came back with a bowl of ice cream just for her.

"My brother had two loves—but there was less pain because all the parents were in agreement and so—"

"Shut up, Ravi. Just shut up or I'll kill you," Nancie said.

The movie-star brother was afraid of his mother, I thought. Nancie had been so happy once. I could still see her the day after I'd arrived, when she'd sneaked out of bed and showed me her scrapbook, hers and Dino's. The most beautiful girl in the world, I'd thought. Was that less than four months ago?

Nancie proved right about one thing, though. Not a week passed before Dino's mother came around, looking for the ring.

13

SURE ENOUGH, four days later on the first sunny day in a week, Dino's mother came. Dad calls her a little dumpling of a woman and Boris calls her the dwarf. Anyhow, she had a shopping bag full of calla lilies wrapped in wet newspaper.

"Lilies are for funerals," Nancie said.

"Nancie, my daughter forever," Dino's mother said. "Dino's a good boy but weak like all the men in our family. What a time I've had with his father."

"So where is Dino?"

"Hawaii. Honeymoon. I have to accept, what else can I do? I'm asking you, *amore*?"

This much I could understand, even in Italian, because Nancie'd been teaching me and she said eavesdropping's good practice. I also knew Nancie and Dino had planned to go to Hawaii on their honeymoon. I couldn't see Nancie's face because the curtain was pulled between us but I wasn't surprised by her war whoop.

"Don't you *amore* me!" Nancie said, switching into English. "You've tried to break us up ever since the day you heard I had tuberculosis. Every week Dino told me the rotten stuff you'd say—I wouldn't be strong enough to carry his babies, let alone raise them. He'd have a family of tubercular children, he deserved better. How did I stand three years of that baloney? And now you've won. *Amore*, hell! My blood's on your hands—" Nancie gasped and started coughing.

Then, while Nancie was still gasping for breath, the old lady asked quietly, as if she hadn't heard a word Nancie'd said, "Nancie, *amore*, would it be too much trouble to show me about where it was you threw that ring? Not that I blame you one bit. Dino's been a dog, as you say. He had it coming, and what self-respecting girl would want his ring? But, *amore*, that ring was my grandmother's and I saw in a dream last night I should give it to the church, so could you—"

"I'm on bed rest," Nancie said.

"Then just point."

"No."

"For the church, *amore*?"

Nancie didn't answer. She'd probably turned her face to the wall the way she did with me, because pretty soon Dino's mother walked past my bed, dressed in her rain boots and a pair of overalls she'd brought in her shopping bag. She'd come prepared.

I didn't get to watch her hunt, though. Just as Dino's mama left, my old boyfriend, Mike, walked in.

"Happy New Year," he said casually.

I'd had four postcards, one a month, asking me to his senior prom. Plus a Christmas card and a stuffed cougar. If he wasn't the very last person in the world I expected to see, he was near the bottom of the list.

"Why didn't you write to me, April?" He grinned a little uneasily.

I shrugged. I don't know why I didn't write, except that every time I started a letter to Mike I got this guilty feeling about having TB, a "look at April and *die*" feeling. "I wrote but I tore them up. Does your mother know you're here?"

"I got to missing you so bad I had to come."

I tried to smile. But the sheer vitality of him made me want to reach for dark glasses. Mike was six-three, big-boned, blue-eyed, and suddenly showing up here, by my bed, he looked like some Viking giant.

"Mind if I sit for a spell?" He handed me a bunch of daffodils, obviously pleased with my astonishment.

"Why didn't you tell me you were coming?"

"I wanted to start the New Year right. Glad to see me?"

"I guess. It's been a while, but—yes—I'm glad."

"Countin' every hour to see the most beautiful girl in California."

Mike and I looked at each other. I was damning my dirty hair and lack of makeup. He was probably wondering what had possessed him to come. He leaned over to kiss me and then—suddenly—jerked back as if he'd been bitten by a rattler. I didn't blame him, but it wasn't much fun either.

"Not like the good old days," I said.

"So glad to see you, I almost forgot TB."

I shrugged. What could I say? Talking had never been our strong point. We'd been competitive swimmers, and rehashing meets would somehow lead to landing us in each other's arms. That was taboo now. So I waited for him to start.

"How's it going, April?"

There was concern in his eyes. I must look terrible.

I smiled. "You look great, like a Viking."

Actually, he was so muscled he was almost too much. I was used to Ravi's small-boned cat man look. Ravi would love the Viking crack, but Mike didn't even smile. The only thing here that would interest him was that I'd met Ravi.

He looked around, taking in the long-stemmed roses, Scheherazade in her cage, the box of chocolates. If only I could slip into Aunt Gretchen's French negligee, then maybe I'd look romantically ill and he couldn't resist kissing me. Things were always easier for Mike and me after we'd kissed.

"Ra-vi. Ra-vi," chirped Scheherazade. One of three words the bird knew.

"Guess it's trying to say 'April,' " Mike said.

"A-pril, A-pril, A-pril," trilled the parakeet, clear as day. She knew what she was saying.

"So okay, bird! Do you like it here, babe? Are they good to you? When you coming home?"

"Miss me?"

He grinned and I grinned and we began to get a little connection. So I told him about Monday fluoroscoping and my roomie breaking up with her fiancé. But soon I noticed his attention shifting to his flowers, not yet in water.

"I'll put them in with the roses until one of the nurses brings a vase," I said, sticking them in with roses four times their height. "I love daffodils," I added quickly.

"Who sent you roses?"

"Oh, an Indian prince who wants to marry me," I said, trying to sound offhand.

Mike laughed hilariously. "Sure thing. And now you have daffodils from the King of England. Must get lonely here, huh?"

"Not really. Scary maybe, but not lonely." Mike shifted uneasily. He didn't want to hear about scary. He shivered and frowned at all the open windows.

"Open windows are part of Dr. Shipman's cure," I told him.

"How about if I close them?" he asked.

"Sure." I glanced at my watch. It was getting close to time for Ravi's exercise. Ten minutes. While I'd love Mike to see that there really *was* an Indian prince, I didn't want Ravi to think Mike was competition.

"How're things at school?"

"I had the best breaststroke time on the swim team,

so I'm in for the all-city meet. Karen, the kid who took your place in freestyle, isn't the swimmer you are by a mile. It's not the same without you, babe."

"Congratulations. I wasn't so good at the last." But I was distracted, wondering how to head off Ravi. Strange. I'd cried my eyes out over Mike when I first got here. And it still hurt when I remembered us walking down the hall at school or swimming or dancing together. But now?

I had this crazy urge to lean over and kiss him and see how it felt, compared to Ravi. Then I heard Mike asking if I'd be out in time for the senior prom.

"You think this is a spa or something? How do I know when I'll be well? You want to ask someone else, go ahead."

"It's just that I'm graduating."

"Go ahead! Mike, see Mount Tamalpais? Do you remember climbing up there on V-E day? I look at it every day."

"And miss me?"

"Maybe." Then, suddenly, I felt a tickling in my throat, a coughing spell coming on, and I panicked—coughing and choking and reaching blindly for water, all the time kicking myself for making it worse. If I could only relax, this would pass. Mike gave me one horrified look and ran for a nurse.

Of course he found Mary Jane and she forced water down me and beat me on the back, giving the impression this was a regular stunt, part of my repertoire.

"Nothing to worry about, just too much company," Mary Jane said.

So Mike jumped to his feet and by the time I was really myself again, he was edging toward the door.

"I'll be back, don't worry," he said.

"Or she could be allergic to the parakeet," Mary Jane added.

Just at that moment Ravi pushed open the door. He looked Mike over, sat down in the chair by my bed, reached out and took my hand in his. "Easy, princess."

Mike turned and stared. Then, as if he'd never thought of leaving, he walked back over and sat on the foot of the bed.

"Introduce me," he said.

"Mike, this is Ravi—from India."

Mike looked at my roses and raised an eyebrow. He saw Ravi holding my hand and cuddled my feet through the blanket. "I just came by to ask my girl to the senior prom," he said.

"Or someone else," I muttered. Ravi pressed my hand.

"Ah," said Ravi with a big smile, "you must be the old boyfriend. I am glad to make your acquaintance." He let go of my hand and reached out to shake Mike's.

"It's three months to the dance—you'll be out," Mike said to me as he shook Ravi's hand.

"You are swimmer, a Tarzan of the movies," added Ravi, looking at the little daffodils stuck in with his tall roses. "It is to be expected—another man in love with such beauty—but I, Ravi Bannerjee, live in the castle with the princess."

"April's gonna shed this place soon. You live in India, Ravi?"

Mike caressed my feet through the blankets. Ravi hung on to my hand. I smiled from one to the other, pushing myself with my free hand so I was sitting up against the pillows, where I felt more like a princess and less like a disputed bone. I saw Ravi glance at his watch. He didn't want to leave first, but he couldn't overstay exercise. Mike sure wasn't leaving. I kind of liked this.

Mary Jane came back with fresh water pitchers. "Okay, visiting hours are over, you guys. What do you think you're doing on April's bed? You want to catch TB or what?"

Mike bolted up and said he wasn't asking anyone else to the senior prom. "I'm counting on you. I'll be back, babe," he added on his way out.

Ravi sighed. "And the faithful Scheherazade stands guard night and day," he said, cooing to the bird.

"She kept saying your name while Mike was here."

"For this, I teach her." He opened the cage. The parakeet hopped right onto his hand and made her way up his arm until she perched on his shoulder. "Ra-vi, Ra-vi, Ra-vi," she chirped, as if declaring the winner.

It wasn't until later, when I was twisting and turning, trying to get comfortable enough to fall asleep hours after lights out, that memories of Mike and me came back to haunt me. I'd been lying flat all day, and every bone in my body was bored with every inch of this bed. Ravi called these moments opening the gates to truth, because we're half asleep and can't control what we're thinking. Midnight memories.

Mike and I had gone swimming in the Russian River. Then we had sat on the bank and talked. Mike was going to be a lawyer, and I was going to be a reporter with my own byline. Mike picked wild daffodils and handed them to me, and then I chased him until we collapsed in each other's arms behind a lilac bush. That day I saw my future so clearly. But now I was just drifting by like a branch in the river.

Enough. I snapped on my light, pushed up against the pillows and reached for my book.

"You're not asleep either?" Nancie asked, her light going on. "I've been lying here thinking about Dino's mother. Thank God she didn't find my ring. That greedy pig."

14

Ravi and I had gotten so close and happy with each other that for a while I'd almost accepted lying in bed month after month, taking the cure. We would read the same books, play with the parakeet and I'd count the hours until Ravi's exercise period and his next after-hours appearance. But Mike's visit brought back my life before TB. In the weeks afterward I took a good hard look at life in C Ward. I was moldering away! Ravi was a love, but would we ever even go out on a date?

I'd already had a bad feeling about Nancie ever since the night Dino had told her he was married and about to become a father. She'd turned her face to the wall the way Mom had sometimes, and I didn't like to think about that. Look where it got Mom. And that coward Dino must have known what he'd done because he never came back.

One morning Nancie forbade us to mention his name.

"You have to choose him or me," she said.

"Sometimes I feel like you're not here for me to choose." I wasn't taking much guff since Mike's visit.

"Well, neither is he, so tough beans, right?"

I wanted to tell her it really was tough beans because I'd lost my best friend and still had to live with her. I wanted to tell her I'd told Mom about Dino and her, and Mom had written back that no man was worth risking your life over. But Nancie was skin and bones, less than a hundred pounds, and she coughed if she tried to talk. So I shut up. Nancie got fluoroscoped only once a month now, and someone had to carry her up the two flights of stairs. She kept asking Dr. Shipman to let her go home.

"I don't want to spend another spring in this lousy hospital," she'd told him again when he stopped by after surgery that day.

"You'll go home when you're on an hour's exercise, young lady, and I'll dance at your wedding yet," he snapped.

"No. You know it, too, Doctor. Let me go home."

"You're better off here where we can help you. I've invested too much effort in your health for you to let me down now, Nancie."

"Such an ego. Think of me for a change. Think what's become of me here." Nancie's laugh ended in a sob.

Dr. Shipman looked as if she'd hit him, but he simply patted her hand and left.

As I told Ravi, it sounded as if Dr. Shipman was hearing Nancie's confession when he did his rounds these days. He'd close the curtains around her bed and sit in there for half an hour, their voices rising and falling, rising and falling, too soft to distinguish more than an occasional word.

"But what do you talk about for so long?" I'd ask when he'd gone. I was lucky to get five minutes with him.

"Oh, life, mostly. Things we'd do over if we could—"

"Like what?" I wanted to hear what the Great Man would do over.

But Nancie only laughed.

"At least I made you laugh." I could have bitten off my tongue. Her laugh stopped in midair.

Hour after hour the only sound in our room was Scheherazade's chirping. Silence was getting on my nerves in a big way. I think I would have flipped out if Ravi hadn't come during his exercise every afternoon.

Ravi was teaching my parakeet to say "doctor," and was she practicing! With each new word, she'd chirp and chirp and sound miles away from any human sound and then, suddenly, out it would come, clear as a bell. Then she'd ruffle her feathers and peck at the cage door, demanding to be let out for a reward.

Meanwhile, the week after our New Year's party and without saying a word to anyone, the Mayor of China-town had gone down to surgery and had the terrible lobectomy, the operation Dr. Shipman wanted Nancie to have. They cut out the diseased lower lobe of his left lung. He survived and a month later he came in to visit us—on twenty minutes' exercise!

"It's not so bad. All during the operation I'm awake and I hear everything. Dr. Shipman is sawing my rib while he talk about football. He likes navy team but they do not win, never win championship. And now the sick place in my lung is gone forever. I'm healthy as my great-grandson."

"Nancie, he's seventy years old and he'll be going home soon," I said after Mr. Wu left. "He's well now. Why not have the surgery?" After all, she didn't have to worry what Dino would think anymore.

"You worry about your lungs, kid, and I'll take care of mine, okay?" Nancie said in that new abrupt way she'd acquired. "You don't know everything, even if you think you do."

Mary Jane, who was carrying in fresh water pitchers, gave me one of her sour looks. "She's too weak for surgery," she whispered. "Incidentally, how's your temperature?"

"Up a little, one-oh-one," I admitted. She made me feel guilty about having a temperature, so I added, "It's up in spite of staying flat as a pancake on this stupid bed since the beginning of time!"

"Now you know how I feel," Nancie said.

"Well, neither of you have bedsores, so don't complain," said Mary Jane, taking my pulse. "How do you feel?"

"A little dizzy, that's all."

"Fast pulse," she said, and went out the door.

"Some nurse!"

"What can they do?" Nancie asked.

Then one sunny afternoon in February we saw Dino's mother hobbling along down on the slope beneath our room, rooting around for the engagement ring again. This made Nancie sit up and shake her fist.

"You can't have my ring. Dino gave it to me. Grave robber!"

Nancie could only whisper, and the old lady didn't look up. She didn't come up to visit Nancie after she'd hunted, either.

"You would like if I have her arrested for trespassing?" Ravi asked, probably getting his big idea right then and there.

The next night after lights out, on his fifteen-minute visit, Ravi was kissing me when he suddenly started laughing.

"So now I'm hilarious? Thanks a lot."

"Look, my little orchid."

I recognized Nancie's diamond ring in the palm of his hand, even by the light of a half moon. "Where?"

"I fear that the so selfish mother of Dino might find Nancie's ring. So I pay the gardener to weed out the poison oak and while he is doing this he earns triple if he brings me this ring and, fortunately, he is an honest man. My Valentine present to Princess Nancie."

"But not on Valentine's Day when Nancie's mourning Dino!"

"Not to worry. With this ring—how you say—she has the last laugh."

Ravi is, as Dad says, the hopeless romantic of all time and I couldn't change his mind.

Valentine's Day dawned clear and warm. One of those lovely false spring days. In the hillside gardens across from the hospital, plum trees were blooming, and I yearned to lie under one and let the blossoms drift over me. Ravi and Mike both sent me long-stemmed red roses. Ravi said a man who needed competition to make him generous would always be unfaithful.

Mike's note said: "To my valentine. I understand that you need a diversion in the hospital. But we'll be together again soon. Think senior prom. All my love, Mike." He hadn't said when he'd visit again, but on the whole, I agreed with Dad that this was a "red-letter" Valentine's day.

The owner of the hospital had been playing Chopin waltzes on Nancie's grand piano in the house below. She played well, and I loved listening. I intended to learn to play first thing when I got well. Dad said he'd get me a piano if I promised to learn Beethoven's Moonlight Sonata.

Nancie's company came promptly at two. First her mother and even her father came, for the first time, though he's afraid of tuberculosis and cried when he saw how thin she was.

"You look like my poor mama now," he said.

"Let me come home, Papa. Let me come home for my birthday."

"The doctor said no."

"So, he's the head of our family now?"

"It would be cheaper, Joe," her mother said.

"All right. Enough. We'll talk to that doctor again, Nancie. We'll see, baby."

Then her parish priest came in. He'd been coming more often lately, which I thought was a bad sign, though Mrs. York said he only reminded us to pray for Nancie.

I heard Nancie ask her mother if Dino has a son. He does.

Ravi had an hour's exercise, and he'd been reading love poems from the Baghavad Gita aloud. He had the idea we should be writing poems to each other. Those he read aloud were supposed to teach us how to write, except that he kept losing his place. He was really listening for Nancie's company to leave so he could take her the ring.

Finally Nancie said her goodbyes and everyone trooped out past us.

Ravi leaped up.

"Don't make a big deal out of it," I warned him.

He looked hurt. He pulled back the green curtain between our beds. Nancie was lying on her back with her eyes closed, resting.

"Nancie," he whispered.

"Later, Ravi," she said.

"Only one little moment, princess."

She smiled and nodded, opening one eye. "What's up?"

"I found something of yours," Ravi said softly, and walked over to her bed. Without saying anything more, he opened her hand and closed it around the ring.

I held my breath.

"You know, I've been missing this little critter," Nancy said with a big smile, pushing herself up in bed and slipping the ring back on the third finger of her left hand. "Thanks, Ravi. I've been thinking I'd like to be buried with this—it's meant so much."

By this time I was crying, of course, but careful not to make a sound.

Ravi, however, answered as if this were why he'd given her the ring. "Yes, a favorite possession, to ease you on your journey to the next world," he said softly.

What I kept wondering was, how could Ravi have

known Nancie wanted the ring back, when she wouldn't even let us mention Dino's name? And when Dino used to come visiting her, even if he was two-timing Nancie, at least he'd visit and say he loved her, which was better than the way things were now, wasn't it? Ravi'd been right about that, too. How did he know these things?

Sometimes he really surprised me, this guy, even now, as well as we knew each other.

15

O NE GLOOMY FOGGY MORNING about a week later, I heard Nancie sobbing, great gulping sobs, no silent tears this time. Breakfast trays had been cleared, but the green canvas curtain between our beds was still drawn. I'd hemorrhaged again and was on strict bed rest, so I hesitated. Then I eased out of bed and went over to Nancie. I put my arms around her to hug her and flinched when I felt her arms, the skin so loose that my hands were clasping bones, as if I'd grabbed hold of a skeleton.

"Kid, get back to bed, they'll boil you in oil," Nancie said, but she clung to me.

And it felt good. As if we were still friends, were in this together. Lately I'd wondered, looking at her back as she turned to the wall day after day. We sat on her bed, Nancie and I, hanging on for dear life, while she cried.

"I'm so afraid," she said finally. "So Goddamned afraid."

"Aren't we all!"

"Dr. Shipman told me I was trying to die for revenge. I asked him, how crazy can you get? It was just too hard without Dino. But he was right. I didn't realize till the other day. Mama told me Dino had a little boy and I said, 'He'll be thinking of his kid and forget about me lying here.'

" 'Let's hope so,' Mama said, and I knew she was right. He'd better be thinking of his son.

"And then, since your Ravi gave me back my ring, I've been lying here looking at Dino's diamond back on my finger and feeling good. You know? In spite of everything. Remembering. Thinking over our good times. And we had our share. Suppose Dino was the one lying here, I would have met someone else in three years. Sure, I would. I was a devil. Too bad I can't tell him there's no hard feelings. Maybe you'll tell him for me?"

"Oh, no, Nancie, oh, no."

"Oh, yes, April, oh, yes. I've made myself weak as a kitten. What can I do?"

"Eat. You can have any food you want from my tray."

"No. I want Mama's cooking. It may be too late, but good Italian cooking's my best chance—if I can only get home before my birthday."

"Nancie, don't say 'too late'—it's bad luck—no, no,

no." I was standing by the bed stamping my feet, and Nancie was looking down at those bare feet stamping a concrete floor, and suddenly it struck us both as funny. Who knows why?—but things do that to us here. So we started laughing.

That's why neither of us heard the door open. When we looked up there was Dr. Shipman, so mad his face was purple, and of course, right behind him, Mary Jane.

"I thought you ought to know, Doctor. With a hemorrhage just this week, she's out of bed, pestering poor Nancie," said Mary Jane in that simpering voice she used with him. Her eyes sparkled. She'd done me, and she knew it.

"I called her," Nancie said, and started to cough.

"April, get to bed. I'll take care of you later!" Dr. Shipman bellowed at me, then bent over Nancie, massaging her skinny shoulders. "Easy, easy does it, Nancie. Easy now."

"In bare feet, too," Mary Jane added, pursing her lips, handing the doctor a glass of water for Nancie. But he glared at her. She'd gone too far.

"That will *do*. That's *all*, thank you, Nurse." Reluctantly she backed out, letting the door slam behind her.

Thursday was surgery day. Mary Jane must have seen me and caught Dr. Shipman as he was coming out of surgery. Only last week someone upstairs was thrown out of the hospital for visiting another patient. And he wasn't even on strict bed rest. I felt sick to my stomach. But, but, but—Nancie had needed me, needed me to put my arms around her and listen. And something stubborn sprang up in me, scared as I was. She needed me, and that was what mattered. She was my friend!

Dr. Shipman had drawn the curtain between our beds again, but I could hear Nancie telling him, "I don't want to die. If you really want to dance at my wedding, let me go home. Mama will fatten me up. But hurry, before my birthday, before it's too late."

"And when you cough—or hemorrhage?"

"Hire us a nurse."

Suddenly he snapped back the curtain between our beds.

"What do you think, April? Should Nancie go home?"

I nodded, trying to read his expression. Was there the tiniest twinkle in his eyes, was that possible?

"When's your birthday, Nancie?"

"March seventh. Doctor, did you ever notice how many people die around their birthdays? Your energy's lowest then, is why."

I held my breath, expecting the doctor to have a fit about old wives' tales, but he didn't say a word, just stood there, looking at Nancie. Finally he sighed.

"All right, Nancie, since your roommate's so anxious to get rid of you, I'll talk to your parents. We'll see what we can work out."

"At last," was all Nancie said.

"And now, April," he said, coming over to my bed. "What on earth am I to do with you? You're losing weight, hemorrhaging, and running around the hospital as if we're some sort of Grand Hotel. Barefoot."

"I am not. This is the only time I've been up, and Nancie needed me."

"And if not Nancie, it's Ravi, or Mike's sitting on your bed. Or you need another book or to wash your hair." Dr. Shipman frowned and looked into my eyes. "How am I to get you well again unless you help, my girl?"

"That's not true! I've never even seen Ravi's room! Mike was here one time. Nancie was crying! I lie here day after day until every bone in my body is bored! I hate it and I hate your spy system, too!"

"Every bone is bored? Then bed rest doesn't seem to do the trick, does it? Nancie, what do you think?"

"She never gets out of bed."

"You've been here about five months, April? Slipping bit by bit, and yet there isn't that big a spot. Only a little nickel-sized hole over an air vent." He seemed to be thinking out loud. "Your father called yesterday. He feels you're 'losing ground,' was the way he put it. He makes me toe the line, that dad of yours. Well, there is a way—and it may be the surest bet for the likes of you and me. Gave me a life. We could take that little piece of lung—and you'd never have to worry again." He laid his hand on my shoulder and nodded, still looking into my eyes.

"Mary Jane hates me," I said, unable to think about what he was saying.

"She only wants you to get well."

"No, she hates me."

"No, but she is jealous. Think about the surgery, April. Talk it over with that father of yours." He took his hand off my shoulder and left the room, giving us the oddest little salute before closing the door. A sad gesture, somehow. A vulnerable look on his face.

"Do it," Nancie said fiercely after he left. "Don't be a fool. Do it!"

"I thought he was going to kick me out," I said, but I was thinking that nobody would ever marry me with a scar like a new moon carved down the length of my back. I'd be an old maid. And hunched over, too. "You wouldn't do 'it,' Nancie. *You* wouldn't."

"Sure, do what I do, kid. Works out great, huh? What a role model. Or maybe you'd prefer that baseball player upstairs? He wouldn't have the operation 'cause he didn't want to wreck his throwing arm, and now Mrs. York says he's dying. Don't wait too long. Dr. S. used to say 'dime-sized spot,' and now it's 'nickel-sized.' "

I covered my ears. Surgery. Lobectomy. *Lobectomy*. "Dad will never allow it," I said firmly. Then, after Nancie didn't answer, "It's because the doctor doesn't know what else to do," I said, suddenly knowing what that farewell salute of his meant. Defeat. "He wants to think I'm up running around, that it's my fault I'm not getting better, because he doesn't know how to cure me." Oh, Lord! If that were true, what then?

Ever so slowly Nancie sat up and dangled her feet over the edge of her bed, using her hands to hold herself steady. What did she think she was doing?

"Listen," she said, and her voice was hoarse, hardly a whisper. "And don't smart-alec me, April. I haven't the energy. All I know is the Mayor of Chinatown is seventy years old and he had it and now he's walking out of here with more years left than either of us has. Think about it, think about him."

"You can't say its name either."

"Lobectomy. It's only a word."

"No one would love me, Nancie. No one would marry me with a new moon carved across my back like Zorro's revenge," I whispered. I'd told her Dino wouldn't care. I'd been crazy in the head. Mike would throw up.

"Ask Ravi. I dare you. Anyhow, who cares about a scar? You'll get well. You'll have your life back. Okay?"

"I couldn't swim anymore."

"Dr. Shipman swims every morning."

"Championship swimming," I said, dripping sarcasm.

"You can't compete if you're dead, either."

"Thanks, pal." I plumped my pillows and turned away, turning my back on Nancie.

16

"LOOK, RAVI, someone went home," I said, nodding toward an empty room as we stood in the fluoroscope line the following Monday morning. The bed was crisply made up and waiting.

"The baseball player died Friday evening. Boris said it is a waste. It was not necessary that he die."

"Died! Oh, no. I hate it! He was—your age, Ravi." My voice dropped to a whisper as I saw others in line staring. I couldn't look at them. Their sad, skinny faces showed too much sympathy.

"It is the will of the gods and we only accept," Ravi said gently.

"Then why try?"

"To attract their favor to ourselves, beautiful one."

I shook my head. "Fat chance. Not here." How could I have been so stupid? Of course, it was the baseball player's room! Next to Eleanor, the astronomer. That wonderful teasing grin he had. Gone forever! I never even knew his name. He was dying when Nancie was telling me to get surgery so I wouldn't end up like him. Or her. He was always waving and joking when I came by. He'd wanted to be friends and so had I. But we'd only passed in the hall.

"He didn't look so sick," I whispered to Ravi. "That's the trouble with this place. We know all the gossip about each other but we can't become friends because we're on bed rest and the next thing you know the guy's dead."

"Your turn soon, my April. The good doctor will put you on exercise next."

Little did Ravi know what the good doctor had in mind for me. I shrugged. What could I say?

"Made it in the nick of time," Dad said, rushing up when I was next in line for fluoroscope.

"The baseball player died," I said flatly.

"Oh, I'm sorry," Dad replied, his face serious.

Ravi's face paled when he came out of fluoroscope and saw Dad. His eyes held mine. He knew Dad's being here meant bad news. Still, he was gracious.

"We are honored by your presence, sir."

"Thank you, Ravi," Dad replied, nudging me toward that steel door.

Ravi blew me a kiss.

Inside, the doctors also pretended Dad was honoring us.

"Just wanted to see that dime-sized spot you all keep telling me is raising such a commotion," Dad said.

"Hope you're not disappointed." Dr. Clark's laughter at his joke echoed in our silence.

Dr. Shipman arranged the mirrors so Dad and I could see my heart and lungs and pointed out the chalky hole in the lower lobe of the right lung. Suddenly he asked, "How does it look to you, April?"

"The size of a nickel now," I whispered.

"Afraid so," said Dr. Clark.

Later, on the way downstairs, Dad said this was the first time he'd ever seen anyone's heart and lungs at work and he'd gotten so dizzy he was afraid he might pass out and disgrace me.

"But isn't it out of the frying pan and into the fire, Doctor? April's only sixteen," Dad said an hour later, when he and the two doctors stood around my bed. "She's got her whole life ahead of her—and this cavity is such a little hole, only a problem because it's over an airhole, right? Surely a few more months in bed is preferable." Dad spoke quietly, but there was a "don't try to push me" tone in his voice.

"What's the hurry, Sid?" asked Dr. Clark, puffing out his cheeks in the squirrel-like way he had.

I was worrying about Ravi. He'd looked as if someone had socked him when he saw my father at the fluoroscope room. He knew I'd been keeping bad news from him.

"Well, April, what do you say? Yes or no?" Dr. Shipman suddenly turned those intense gray eyes on me.

"Don't intimidate the girl, Sid."

"Not possible, Bob. This is a girl who knows her own mind, don't you, April? The thing is, she could be free."

"And have less lung power the rest of her life," my father said quietly.

"Doesn't slow me down," snapped Dr. Shipman. He was still looking at me as if he expected me to decide, to speak up and convince my father. But Dad was right about less lung power.

"Would I still be able to swim?"

Dr. Clark gave me a mournful look and patted my foot, then left to continue his rounds. But my father and Dr. Shipman stood there, frowning at each other. My stomach was churning.

"I swim every morning, April." Dr. Shipman turned back to Dad and began talking as if I'd said "Sure, go ahead." He explained the cost of the surgery, after-effects, side effects, the danger of doing nothing. The mortality rate at my age was not much more than ten percent under local anesthesia. One in ten you were dead? Not all that great.

Dad listened without interrupting. He was silent after the doctor finished.

Finally Dr. Shipman cleared his throat.

"Well," said Dad after a pause, "let's wait two

months, see how the lung looks then, and take another look at our options."

"Your daughter, your decision, sir. We'll meet here in two months, then." They shook hands, and Dr. Shipman left.

"He's angry," I said after the door swung shut behind him.

"I'm looking out for your life, April, not his pride."

I nodded. We were quiet awhile. "Well," I said finally, "I guess I'd better write and tell Mike I won't be his senior prom date."

"Not too likely," Dad agreed, and then he grinned. "Well, it's one letter to Mike that Ravi should be happy about."

I couldn't help grinning back, though I was pretty sure it meant the last I'd hear from Mike. There were no proms in C Ward. And after Dad had gone I did write to Mike, all of about four lines, and sealed and stamped the note quickly. Then I had a flash of how I would feel lying in this bed another year, maybe two. Every muscle would be screaming "Go!" Ravi would be back in India. Didn't my father care how long I rotted in this bed? Didn't the doctor care if I died during surgery?

Nancie must have heard every word through the curtain, but she didn't say anything, and neither did I. What was the point? They'd shelved the surgery for two months. Maybe Ravi'd never have to know. I'd say Dad wanted to see the lung because I'd been hemorrhaging. And that was true. I had two months to get well. I'd do it.

For a week, Nancie seemed better. She was skinny and her skin looked transparent, but you could hear her laugh again and that made all the difference. She was so happy to be going home at the end of the month—just before her birthday—home until she gained fifteen pounds.

Then suddenly one night her temperature went shooting up and her cough was bad, really bad, that scary choking cough that made you feel as if you were strangling.

Boris came in and gave her a backrub, then sat with her until she dozed off. When he left, he asked me to let him know if she had any more trouble. Anything at all. "Ring your bell at the first moment," he said.

"Suppose I fall asleep?"

"Oh, please, yes, sleep. Only if you wake up and you hear."

"Okay."

But who could sleep with Boris coming in every few minutes? And Nancie moaning in her sleep. Her throat rattled with each breath. It sounded like snoring, except that I'd only heard this hoarse rattle once before, the night the Irishman, Irving, had died.

"Nancie, are you okay?" I must have asked a dozen times, but mostly she didn't answer.

Once she did say, "I bless you, kid."

"Nancie, you're the best friend I've ever had."

"Thanks."

I must have fallen asleep in spite of myself, because the next thing I heard was Nancie calling "Dino, Dino," in a terrible croaking whisper.

Then someone came in with Boris, and I recognized Dr. Clark's voice. Boris woke him up to come in the middle of the night! Oh, God, it must be serious.

I heard the call of an owl, shrill and filled with warning, again and again. It had been raining earlier and the sky was black and empty. No moon. No stars. Just Nancie six feet away, breathing as if each effort might be her last. I breathed with her, in and out, in and out, gulping air, trying to help.

I'd broken out in a cold sweat. My teeth were chattering, and fear crept slowly up my arms and legs, paralyzing me inch by inch. I couldn't even scream, though I wanted to scream at Nancie, "Don't give up, not when you're going home! Your mother will fatten you up and you'll be okay."

"Hang in there. It's not your birthday for a whole week," I whispered.

"She asked for a priest and I called him," I heard Boris say.

"All right." Dr. Clark's voice was testy. "How long ago?"

"He come anytime now."

"Let's hope so. She's slipping into coma."

Oh, God, I couldn't stand this. Why did I have to listen to this? I was freezing and needed another blanket, but I didn't want them to know I was awake. I don't know how long I lay there, cold and afraid and shivering. I heard the priest come and go, his leather soles on the concrete louder in the dark silence than his prayers had been. Nancy didn't speak. Did she know he'd come?

Dr. Clark left too. I saw him go out the door and realized I must have dozed again because it was getting light, that first flat gray light that only birds and insomniacs like me see. Nancie? But Boris was still with Nancie, so she must have made it. I could hear him murmuring to her softly in Russian.

"Boris," I called.

"Shhh, she sleeping."

"Thanks."

I drifted off to the song of birds and the smell of Ravi's roses. We'd gotten through that long night. All right. All right!

When I woke again it was raining and I thought, The sky is crying for Nancie. It was broad daylight, but there was no sound and no nurses or doctors were at the other bed. Somehow, I knew she was gone. I sat bolt upright and slipped out of bed, instantly awake. I wanted to see her once more, even if— As I walked around that green canvas curtain, I knew she'd look as if she were sleeping. Maybe she *was* only sleeping!

But she was gone! Gone! The bed had been freshly made, corners pulled tight and flat, flat, flat. There was no one in that bed. For a moment I wondered if Nancie had gone home. I remembered that squeaking gurney. I wouldn't have slept through that, surely? I stood there staring at that clean white bed. I needed to see Nancie, to lay my hand on her arm. They'd deliberately taken her away from me—but why? Why, when I needed her so?

"Nancie, oh, Nancie," I whispered.

I was still standing there at the end of her bed when Dr. Shipman came in. "I thought you might be awake," he said, and led me back to my bed, tucked me in and sat patting my hand. I shook my head and he took his hand away, sitting quietly in the chair where my father and Ravi usually sat.

"Where is she?"

"She's gone, April. In her sleep. Peacefully, without regaining consciousness."

"You didn't bring the gurney?"

"No, a stretcher."

"I want—to see her again." I didn't even feel like crying. "I have to see her again."

"We have to remember her as she was, our Nancie. That's what I have to do, too."

134

"No. You're used to this, and Nancie's the first person I ever loved—who died."

He stood then. "I never get used to it, April. I'm sorry. I loved Nancie too, so I know how tough this is."

"But how can I know without—seeing her?" And it was true. I stayed suspended, without feeling, all day. I watched the doctor leave, the nurses come and go. Ravi tried to comfort me; my father came early and stayed late; but I remained frozen, in shock. Finally I slept.

Sometime during that next long night, I must have gotten out of bed and walked around the curtain and crawled into Nancie's bed. I don't remember that. First thing I knew I was in Nancie's bed and sobbing, and I remember thinking, Oh, Nancie, how could you leave us, after all, when it wasn't even your birthday? Oh, Nancie. And that's where they found me in the morning, in her bed, sleeping soundly, her pillow still wet with my tears.

NANCIE'S MOTHER gave me her pearl earrings. Mrs. York and I cried when she put them in my ears because Nancie'd always worn them. They felt so good. They didn't bring her back, of course, but every time I reached up and touched them, I could hear her laugh again. And they buried her with Dino's ring, just as she'd wanted.

Three days after Nancie died, I got a new roommate. Rena Lewis was in her early twenties, not so much older than Nancie but already a medical doctor. She'd gotten TB from a patient when she was working as an intern. She'd also been married for four months to a handsome man, though she was pretty mousey, the type with thick horn-rimmed glasses and men's striped pajamas. She moved in with a movie projector, twenty-two pelargonium plants, and a bookcase filled with books.

"I hope you like Charlie Chaplin and the Marx

Brothers because I've got them all. April and I are going to laugh ourselves well," she told my father.

"Suppose I bring in some of my footage, too, sometime? I'd like you both to see what we're up to," Dad offered.

"Good. April said you were a screenwriter. How about tomorrow night, seven o'clock?" Rena asked.

"Are you always so definite?"

"I try. Otherwise, whole days dribble away."

"But isn't this supposed to be a rest cure?" Dad's voice was amused and admiring. He obviously liked Rena.

"I doubt boredom ever cured anyone."

So Rena moved in and took over and, most of the time, I was glad to have her. I could only take so much of remembering Nancie. I was on complete bed rest and I needed diversion. Still, it was a shock every time I looked over and saw her lying there in Nancie's bed. I had to remind myself it wasn't Rena's fault she was here instead of Nancie. In fact, she wouldn't have been here at all if she hadn't been helping some patient like Nancie or me.

Within forty-eight hours I'd watched my father's great film about the Southern Pacific Railroad and five of Charlie Chaplin's old movies and had started learning German. Rena wanted me to read *The Magic Mountain*, a novel about life in a tuberculosis sanitarium, in the original German. Thomas Mann's novel was almost a thousand pages long, but as Dad said, a little German wouldn't hurt and I could always finish the book in English.

Dr. Shipman hefted the book and didn't even want me to read it in English. "I hear it's depressing," he said.

"I'll let you know when I finish it."

"Oh, come, come, Doctor," Rena said. "This girl's mind is going to seed. She should be finishing high school, and I'm only doing the best I can to fill in."

"Rena, you'll be more than enough education for April. She needs rest and so do you."

"Nonsense. She needs pleasure and so do you."

To my astonishment, Dr. Shipman laughed.

It turned out that Rena was a certified genius and came from a family of certified geniuses. Her father was a famous doctor and Dr. Shipman had studied with him. That's why Rena got away with murder, according to Mary Jane, who hated Rena even worse than she hated me. Maybe Mary Jane thought Rena was in Nancie's bed, too.

"Eaten up with vile jealousy," Rena said about Mary Jane.

When Rena had been my roommate for about two weeks, she and Ravi discovered they both loved history. Rena suggested we use some of Ravi's exercise time for a history half hour. He would teach us Indian history and Rena would take on the rest of the world. It sounded like fun, but I was surprised at Ravi's enthusiasm, because Rena was already really nosey about his family.

"We'll play Fall of the British Empire and April will be our designated student," Rena said with a grin.

"My beautiful one will see the rise of Mahatma Gandhi," Ravi replied, his eyes sparkling.

Ravi sat between our beds and poured Darjeeling tea from a china teapot. Neither he nor Rena could stand tea bags or heavy hospital dishes.

I had a headachey temperature that first afternoon. This etched some scenes Ravi described forever on my mind and made me forget the rest. I lost hundreds of years of Indian kingdoms. Rena and Ravi were throwing names and dates about like rival historians. I tried to take it all in, but my head felt as if it would split open.

"Where Gandhi leads, I will follow," Ravi was saying, a little pompously if you ask me, even waving the teapot for effect.

"Not to some mildewing prison if you intend to keep sound lungs," Rena replied. "And not on any salt marches to the sea, either."

"Gandhi, our spiritual guide, stands between us and death when the British leave."

"But isn't he like Robin Hood—taking money from rich families like yours to give to the poor?" Rena asked.

"We are honored to give."

"Ravi, I can see that God runs a poor second to Gandhi in your eyes," Rena said, laughing.

"The Mahatma is India."

I thought wistfully of the days when Ravi and I had dribbled away our afternoons. I could hear the echo of Nancie's joyous laugh. Still, I was lucky to have Rena. She wasn't very sick. She had lesions only in one lung, and she didn't even have a cavity. Besides, Rena was what she called "newlywed happy." If only my head didn't hurt! What were they talking about now?

"Mary Jane hates us because we don't weigh two hundred pounds," Rena said.

I pushed myself up painfully to listen.

"Boris says she is a different girl on a date, a happy girl," Ravi insisted.

"Then she should quit and we'll all be happy. Anyway, in India you rather like your women ample, don't you? Even your sisters are on the plump side."

"Mary Jane likes men better than women," I said. Speaking made me realize it wasn't really my head but my jaws that ached. Maybe I had lockjaw.

"My sisters," Ravi replied stiffly. "My sisters are beautiful and ladies betrothed. Bharati will marry next month—very rich man, though a lawyer. One day he will be Mayor of Bombay, they say." Ravi had been insulted. He might stick up for Mary Jane but would not have his adored sisters compared to her. I tried moving my jaws, but the pain was horrendous. Even my teeth ached. Hey, maybe I had a toothache!

"And are you going home for the wedding?"

"Clearly I cannot be traveling, Rena. Unfortunately."

"You look like a healthy young man to me."

"I must recover my tiger strength. My father said this to me on the phone yesterday."

So, he'd talked to his father yesterday. Had Ravi asked to go home for his sister's wedding? Why hadn't he told me? Until Rena came and asked whatever popped into her head, I felt as if he didn't have family.

"What do you want to be, Ravi?"

"When I grow up, Rena?" He laughed, embarrassed. She nodded, looking at him intently. "What university, for starters?"

"Cambridge," he said quietly, not looking at me.

"And then?"

Ravi shrugged and grinned, his usual dodge for serious questions. "I am here and happy. If I think of home, then I waste glorious days in sadness, no?" he said, taking my hand.

"Well, it seems to me I've heard that line before." Rena raised an eyebrow.

I looked away from them, out the window, past hummingbirds fighting over sugar-water feeders, over the hillside homes, to Mount Tamalpais and the wonderful empty sky. A mountain peak shaped like a reclining maiden in a wind-up hospital bed, I thought. Like Nancie in the sky waiting for her Dino.

"Oh, my teeth hurt so much," I said aloud, surprised to hear my voice.

"I thought you looked washed out," Rena said, hopping out of bed. "Open your mouth," she demanded.

Reluctantly I opened. "God in Heaven, what an abscess. Will you keep your mouth open? I have to see. Another one's impacted. Both wisdom teeth."

"Don't sound so happy."

"You, my dear, must go to the dentist. Those have got to come out."

"Fat chance. I'm on bed rest—can't even get up for the john, remember?"

"Trust me," said Rena, and, pulling on her mother's old pink chenille robe, she slipped out the door.

"At least she'll get aspirin," said Ravi. "You should have told us."

"I just figured it out. I've never had a toothache before," I said, wishing Ravi would go so I could just give in and cry. I could hear Rena and Boris talking in the hall, back and forth, back and forth. "I could have had a painkiller by now if I didn't have a doctor for a roommate."

"*Namaste*, peace," said Ravi, taking my hand.

Finally Rena came back, grinning.

"You've an appointment with a dentist in San Rafael tomorrow afternoon, four o'clock. I made the appointment, then called Sid Shipman, and he blustered a bit but authorized the trip. We agreed that you can't get well with abscessed wisdom teeth. You'll go by taxi with Boris."

"And me," said Ravi. "The doctor says I may walk anywhere for one hour."

"I'm going outside?"

"Paroled," Rena agreed.

"I don't believe it."

But I did go. I felt so dazzled walking down the sunny hillside ramp, hand in hand with Ravi and Boris. The gentle sunshine, the teasing spring breeze, the air! Light-headed and lighthearted, I waved to Rena and the others on our floor. And they waved back, just as Nancie and I had to the Mayor of Chinatown when he'd left the hospital. I'd waved with such yearning I'd found my feet walking in bed, in step with his.

There was a dentist who came to the hospital and pulled teeth once or twice a year, but I'd never heard of anyone being treated outside before. And, best of all, my teeth had stopped hurting. The painkillers must have kicked in.

"And we have time for a glass of wine first?"

"Yes, *dushka*, half an hour."

I wanted to stroll down lovely streets, rubbing shoulders with healthy people, singing and dancing, but it was exhausting to walk down our little hillside to a waiting taxi. Boris said he knew a sidewalk café where we could sip wine and watch the world go by. I couldn't have a glass of wine but I could sip a little of his.

We found a table in the sunshine. There were even sweet peas on our table. I leaned over to smell them, secretly watching two young couples at the next table. They were feeding each other french fries, catsup dripping all over the table, the girls giggling and the boys demanding more french fries. Ravi and I smiled at each other.

The girls turned to watch us then, a little jealously, I thought. Ravi was spectacularly handsome since he'd gained weight and gone on exercise. And Boris was the kind of tall, blond older man girls dream about. They thought I had it made! I smiled at the girls and they looked away.

"You were never so loud, so vulgar, my beautiful one," Ravi whispered, wrinkling his nose and taking my hand. Mike and I had played with french fries, but I just smiled. Mike hadn't answered my prom letter. I'd known he wouldn't but I'd hoped he would.

"So sure?" Boris asked. "I think April is devil when she wants to be. Remember New Year's Eve?"

We laughed and toasted our good health, Boris pouring wine into his empty water glass and passing it quietly to me. I glanced at my watch. Only fourteen more minutes of freedom. "Nancie would have loved this," I said, and watched a companionable shadow of sadness pass over the men's faces.

Too soon it was time to go. The dentist would be waiting. My teeth ached again, and I was so tired my hands trembled.

"Do they know how lucky they are?" I murmured, looking at the young couples.

"No, but we do and so we appreciate," Boris said, his hand resting lightly on my shoulder.

"Yes, we will come again when April is on an hour exercise," Ravi promised, gently lifting me to my feet.

"Ah, not yet!" But I rose and left the café, arm in arm with my friends. Ravi handed me a sweet pea.

"For smelling salts," he said.

The nurse was waiting wearing a mask against my contagion. I surrendered myself.

"Your friends remain here, please," the nurse said coldly. She was afraid of me, a tubercular bearing the plague, I thought.

I followed her into a stainless steel cubicle, took the pills she offered, and hoisted myself into the dental chair.

"The doctor will be with you shortly," she said, backing out the door.

My mouth hurt. The wine was making me sick. Or the pills were. Oh, God, don't let me throw up.

The next thing I knew, the dentist was standing over me, dressed for surgery, mask and gown. Nice brown eyes.

"Well, pretty brave girl to fall asleep waiting for the dentist, April," he said, preparing a hypodermic.

"How do you know my name?"

"Saw it on your chart. Open your mouth, please? How did your teeth ever get in this shape?" he asked.

"What shape?"

"One abscessed wisdom tooth and another impacted and there must be a dozen cavities. Do you eat a lot of sweets?"

"I'm tubercular. We eat sweets to gain weight."

"Well, you'll be coming in for months, young lady."

"Don't I wish," I said.

He went on talking while he shoved the needle into my mouth, and when he drove it in around the abscessed tooth I nearly went through the ceiling. But the dentist simply held me down and injected the other side, which I hardly felt because I was so mad.

"It hurts now, but a few minutes more and I'll have them out. Then they'll never hurt you again," he said.

He seemed to speed up like Rena's Charlie Chaplin movies. The icy nurse kept handing him instruments, taking them back and checking my pulse, never taking her eyes off me. Just as he said, almost before I knew it, two teeth were out.

Ravi and Boris were waiting impatiently. Ravi'd used up his hour's exercise. He'd be in trouble if Mary Jane found out.

"The taxi waits downstairs," Boris said gently while Ravi put his arms around me and crooned something that must have been an Indian lullaby.

It wasn't until my father arrived with ice cream that evening and asked how the dentist had gone that I remembered the sidewalk café. The sunshine and sweet peas, the heady feeling of being a pretty girl out with a couple of handsome boyfriends. Admired and envied by other girls.

"Oh, it was wonderful," I told my startled father. "I'll never forget it."

18

DAD DIDN'T STAY long that night. He said I looked like a sorehead, and I said, "Don't make me laugh because it hurts." So we read our newspapers and he patted my shoulder and left. Afterward, I turned off my light and lay in the dark. Maybe Rena thought I'd gone to sleep. At any rate, her curtain was pulled between our beds but not around the bottom. I was lying there half-asleep when I happened to glance up and see her reflected in my bureau mirror. Rena and her husband, Paul.

Paul was leaning over the bed holding her in his arms. They kissed and then he ran little kisses over her face. Rena had her glasses off and she wore a soft lacy negligee. And she was so beautiful, full-breasted and tiny-waisted, like Lana Turner. She didn't even look like our daytime Rena in men's striped pajamas. I closed my eyes and opened them again. Rena was still beautiful and Paul was telling her he loved her. But it was the look on their faces that held me spellbound. They were radiant, both of them! I couldn't get enough of the tender way they looked at each other, as if they'd personally discovered the wonder of love.

There was more whispering, and Paul turned away from Rena and reached over and pulled the curtain around the foot of the bed. Then I heard him sit on her bed. Rena's light snapped off. Suppose another visitor came in? Or Boris?

They sighed and whispered. I could hear their tender happiness and in my mind's eye I saw their faces light up as they looked at each other. I was so jealous I almost hated them. But I didn't. I wanted to be Rena, and I was very much afraid I would never in my whole life have such a love.

Then the whispering got more intense and it wasn't long before Paul called out, "Good night, love, until tomorrow," as he did every night. He came walking right by my bed.

"Good night, April. See you tomorrow," he called.

Rena's light snapped on after he left and she headed for the bathroom. She had on her glasses and her mother's old pink chenille robe again. Rena said buying clothes was a bloody bore and she preferred broken-in soft comfies from the Goodwill.

Still, no matter how you cut it, there wasn't much going on in this hospital that made for radiant faces. Nancie and Ravi had said the baseball player who died and the nurse who got fired had been in love. Nancie and

Dino hadn't ever kissed here as far as I knew. If they had maybe he wouldn't have married that blonde. Maybe Nancie would still be alive. Maybe Dino would be a patient now. What if Mike and I had connected when he'd walked in that day? Or if Ravi and I—suddenly I flushed all over, even started to roll over on my sore jaw. The pain shocked me back to normal.

Rena didn't even glance in my direction when she came out of the bathroom. Maybe she was too happy to remember a roomie's wisdom teeth. She climbed back into bed and opened a book, as usual.

So I lay there, biting my pillow bitterly. I'd never have a man who loved me the way Paul loved Rena, not after a lobectomy. I'd either be scarred for life or I'd die. I'd either be a withered old maid or a young corpse. Some choice.

I brooded for a week. Either way, whether I had a lobectomy and was scarred for life or didn't have it and died like Nancie, I was never going to fall in love and get married and have children the way most people did. Rena and Paul never left the curtain open again and I got over feeling jealous of them and tragic about myself, but those were the facts of life.

Meanwhile, my jaws were healing. When I was weighed the following Monday I'd lost two pounds, but the doctors only said it was lucky I hadn't lost more, considering the looks of me.

"April, your jaws look like you've been KO'd by

Joe Louis," Dr. Shipman said when he took out the stitches.

My face looked worse than it felt. The dentist was right about the pain ending after the extraction. But I hadn't said so because I'd wanted to go back to the dentist's office to get the stitches out. I'd wanted another half hour at the sidewalk café. No such luck.

One morning I was lying in bed trying to decide about the surgery when I got just totally fed up! Totally! I was sick of bedpans and bed baths and running a temperature and coughing and living my whole life from a wind-up hospital bed. Ravi and I had never even been out on a date.

My seventeenth birthday was a week off—April 10. I was on bedpans. A big black cloud called lobectomy hovered on the horizon. And look what had happened to Nancie just before her birthday.

"April, who's that with Ravi?"

Rena's voice jarred me. "Where? Must be someone else. Ravi never has company."

"Over on the path that winds around the hill. Looks Indian to me. Sikh turban."

She was right. Ravi was wearing the orange silk tunic he'd worn New Year's Eve, and the older man was wearing a business suit and a white turban. They walked slowly, talking, sometimes stopping and considering, then walking again. They both looked serious. "I don't know. He didn't say anything about expecting anyone. But he doesn't tell me about the phone calls from his family either, so—who knows?"

"Yes, Ravi's a one-cast-of-characters-at-a-time man," Rena said, raising an eyebrow.

I grinned but watched Ravi thoughtfully. He was in charge out there on the hill. The older man was agreeing with everything Ravi said. And my boyfriend was every inch the prince. He even walked differently, straight ahead and chin up. I was proud of him but it bothered me, somehow. I was watching a stranger.

"Do you think he'll bring his Sikh in to meet us?"

"Not the way I look." My jaws didn't hurt anymore and the swelling had gone down, but I looked like yesterday's facelift. From the nose down I was black, blue and yellow. No, Ravi was not likely to show me off to anyone from India.

"Suppose he does?" Rena asked. "After all, it's history this afternoon and his turn."

"No," I said. "Just no."

Nevertheless, I put on makeup and Aunt Gretchen's lavender negligee, in case. As it turned out, Ravi sent a note saying he regretted the delay of our history hour more than we would ever know but he had permission to go out to an Indian dinner and so would his beautiful friend forgive him until tomorrow?

"Those Indians! I had an Indian lover once," said Rena, laughing.

I blushed and then, to my horror, burst into tears. "I don't want to hear about your lovers, Indian or Paul," I yelled.

Then I sent my dinner back untouched. When Dad came that evening I asked him to go out and get me a hamburger, which he refused to do. First Rena and then Dad asked me what was wrong.

"Nothing!" I shouted. "Just leave me alone."

They did.

Then Scheherazade started chirping nonstop. I threw her night towel over the cage though it wasn't even dark. One last little sad chirp and she shut up. I was feeling that mean.

By the time Ravi arrived the next afternoon, his arms full of Indian delicacies for tea and Kashmir shawls for Rena and me, I was mad enough to spit. It was one of those endless gray, drizzly days. My temperature was up. I wasn't getting any better. The two months were half over.

"Watch out. April's in a throwing mood," Rena told Ravi as he set samosas, puris and mint-scented yogurt out on our bedstand, along with a pretty cloth and a new Indian tea set.

"Throwing roses, I hope," he said, hugging me as he laid the softest white wool shawl, embroidered in blue forget-me-nots, around my shoulders and rested his head against mine for a moment.

"I am in a foul mood," I admitted, feeling a little better at seeing Ravi looking like his usual self again.

"A woman of endless variety. I've never seen my April in a foul mood before," Ravi said, while offering Rena a red wool shawl with a graceful bow.

"Yes, well, lie low today, Ravi," Rena said. "Oh, my, I've never had such a lovely shawl!"

"It's woven by an artist. Thank you," I said, annoyed that Rena had thanked him first.

"I asked our lawyer to bring them from home so I might give myself the pleasure of observing you ladies wearing them."

"We saw you walking with him," I said.

"He's come halfway around the world just to see you?" Rena asked. "Is he staying long?"

"No."

Ravi had a way of saying that one syllable and shutting a subject down, bang. You learned nothing and felt like the busybody of the world. But Rena was stubborn.

"Why did he come?" Rena asked.

Ravi looked up, astonished. "We—had business, nothing of interest. But now—our history lesson. Shall we consider the shawls costumes and pretend you are young ladies of Kashmir, gone houseboating on holiday?"

"I'd like to meet your friend."

"Alas, he has already gone, this morning, Rena, but only a small pity—truly, you would not find him interesting—not friend, only our lawyer—a businessman."

"Why did he come?" I asked.

Ravi turned and stared at me.

"I warned you I was in a foul mood."

And then Ravi's contagious laugh set us all off. "You ladies have—what do you say?—ambushed me. The lawyer is sent by my father, four times a year, to instruct me in the affairs of our principality, since it will be my work to rule one day. I must learn all I can, since I am not natively wise, you see."

"He must be pleased to see you recovered," Rena said.

"So he says." Ravi turned and looked out the window.

I flushed. Rena hopped out of bed and busied herself with the tea. Ravi rolled up my bed and set my cup on the bed table, along with a small plate of samosa and puris. He said nothing. We didn't look at each other. I had invaded his privacy. And for what? These days I didn't want to think about India or his going back there any more than he did. Leave all that over there with the elephants!

But then Ravi did something lovely. He cupped my healing chin gently in his hand and asked, "What is it, my April? Please, share your trouble."

I looked up and his soft brown eyes had so much love, such gentle concern. Oh, I was overwhelmed. I laid my cheek against his. "Oh, Ravi," I said.

"Please, darling, tell me."

Rena pulled her beautiful red shawl around her men's

pajamas and went off to the bathroom, the only way she could give us a little privacy.

There was something so comforting about Ravi. He stood there holding me in his arms, murmuring love words, rocking me a little as I cried myself out and finally rested in his arms. "I'm okay now."

"Then tell me, my beautiful," he whispered.

"Would you—I mean—suppose I had a scar on my back?" Lord knows, I hadn't meant to blurt it out. Without looking at him, I traced the new moon shape on his back so he'd know what I was talking about.

"Oh, my April," he said, tilting my face up to his, looking deep into my eyes, and kissing me. And as he held me tightly, I could see Nancie three months ago, saying, "Ask Ravi, I dare you." We rocked together, his hands caressing my back, my shoulders, my neck, ever so gently.

"Oh, my courageous darling, how could I not love you more? And this scar, a crescent moon, is holy to my people. A sacred tattoo. A new beginning."

"I haven't decided whether to have it, so don't tell anyone, not even Rena," I whispered. "My father's against it. He says I have my whole life ahead of me."

Ravi nodded. "And you?"

"I'm so sick of lying here."

"And sometimes in the night you think of Nancie?"

"Yes. She waited too long." I wanted to tell him how it had felt sitting at the sidewalk café with him, just like anyone else, my vision of getting out of here. But I couldn't. I was too tired, too frightened. It had taken every ounce of strength to say what I had. "It's too hard," I said aloud.

"Too hard," he agreed. He held me, rocking gently, and I almost fell asleep in his arms. We were still holding each other when Rena came out of the bathroom.

"Restores my faith in the human race," she said with a grin.

"Then, shall we have tea and these what you call tidbits from my northern India? Perhaps we learn more from eating than from history this one day, no?"

Rena and Ravi had tea and I lay back, grateful to lie there, listening, half smiling at their soft bursts of laughter. I had to talk with Dad, and soon. Rena, too, but not until I knew what I wanted. A sacred tattoo. A crescent moon. What a sweetheart of a liar. But at least he hadn't run off screaming. And I liked what he'd said about the crescent moon being a new beginning. Maybe so.

19

TELLING RAVI about the surgery was the first step. Going public. I wanted to talk to Rena before tackling Dad and Dr. Shipman again. I had to know, once and for all, would this make me well? I didn't think a crescent-moon scar across my back was sacred. Or that Ravi wanted a wife with one. Baloney. But even so, telling him hadn't been so bad.

And if anyone could give me the straight story, it would be Rena.

"He wants me to have a lobectomy," I said in a rush the next morning over breakfast.

"Shipman's idea or Clark's?" Rena asked, taking a bite of toast.

"Dr. Shipman. He says I'm like him and he got sick again five times before having the operation."

Rena snorted. "Oh, baby! But let me take a look at you in fluoroscope Monday and then we'll talk."

"But what do you think, generally?"

"I never think generally."

"And the scar? I saw an old woman with one in room twelve and her back's hunched up bad."

"Work the arm and brush your hair a hundred strokes a day so you don't atrophy. A scar's only a line on a young body." She shrugged as if it weren't important.

"Rena! Nancie died because she knew Dino wouldn't love her with that scar. I can't be an old maid—please!" The words hung in the air, hitting my ears again and again.

"With your looks? Choosing the right guy's going to be your problem, not a thin line down your back, ladybug. Your Nancie either didn't give her guy credit for brains or she had the wrong man."

I looked at Rena and she met my eyes, nodding slightly, grinning her how-can-you-be-so-dumb grin. Okay. She knew about men and she never believed lying was worth the effort. Suddenly I felt like flying. I'd still be—desirable.

"So, I should do it."

"Hey, let me find out. We'll talk about that after I've seen your lungs and looked over your medical history. Did you talk to Ravi about it? What did he say?"

"Crescent-moon scars are sacred."

Rena started laughing, and suddenly it struck me funny too and we laughed and laughed. "If that boy fell in a creek he'd come up with a fish in his pocket," she said finally, wiping her eyes.

It was only later, after lights out, that I realized why Ravi's reaction had been so endearing and comforting. He was saying courage made the crescent-moon scar sacred.

Rena crowded into the tiny fluoroscope room the following Monday and grabbed hold of the screen and peered hard at my lungs, front and back, with both doctors falling all over themselves trying to answer any questions she might ask before they occurred to her. She stayed on to look at Ravi's lungs, too.

Then she borrowed change from Ravi and me for a long-distance call. "Don't pester me with questions, April. When I know anything sensible, you'll be the first to hear. Meanwhile, let me phone Dad before he goes to lunch."

"Some bedside manner," I said.

"Right."

She talked with her father, Dr. Shipman's surgery professor, for almost an hour, daytime rates. All afternoon she pored over the tuberculosis text Dr. Shipman had loaned her, closing the curtain between our beds, canceling our history hour, reading during supper.

I was a wreck. Suppose I didn't go along with what she said, after all her work? All I'd wanted was her opinion. After all, they were *my* lungs. Knowing how bossy Rena was, I should never have opened my big mouth.

"What's wrong?" Dad asked that evening, perching

Scheherazade on my shoulder so he could clean her cage. Normally she adored Dad but when he cleaned her cage she had a tendency to peck at his hands unless I kept her entertained.

"I asked Rena about a lobectomy and she's—researching, I guess—and won't tell me a thing."

"And you think no news is bad news?"

I nodded.

At that moment Rena ripped back the curtain between us and said, "Done."

"So, what do you think, Rena?"

Dad frowned. "I thought we'd agreed to wait a couple of months and see how you're healing."

I said nothing.

"Didn't we, April?"

"But it *is* almost two months, only three more weeks."

"Don't you want April to have all the facts, Bill?"

Dad put his head in his hands and groaned. When he looked up and nodded, there were tears in his eyes. "I'd hoped she could be spared this," he told Rena.

"Oh, Dad." I couldn't remember ever seeing my father in tears before.

"But why," Rena asked, "should you think surgery's so bad, compared to moldering away in bed?"

"It's the bleeding."

"What bleeding, Bill?"

"Rena, we're talking major surgery. I nearly bled to death at twenty-three just having my tonsils out."

Rena and I stared. "I never knew that, Dad."

"No wonder. Tonsils are barbaric surgery on an adult," Rena said quietly.

"But I won't bleed to death."

"No, you're young, have one good lung yet, and the best surgeon on the coast. The cavity's in a bad spot and growing. Even if it heals, the odds are it will break open again. It's no life for her, Bill."

My heart thumped. "What did your father say?" I asked.

"He thinks you should go ahead. Under local anesthesia."

"Is that what you think, Rena?" Dad asked.

"Yeah, I do."

"Why under local anesthesia?"

"Because the mortality rate is much lower—some twelve percent lower—if she's awake and keeps using her lungs."

I listened to her soft, sure voice rising and falling. They'd take out the lower right lobe. It was going to hurt like hell, and sometimes people stopped breathing right there on the table. That was what mortality rate really meant!

I stopped listening and looked out the window, over to Mount Tamalpais in the gathering dusk. There were drifts of fog and shadow curling together around the summit. I'd miss my view of Mount Tamalpais. But I aimed to be one of those girls at the sidewalk café laughing with a boyfriend. I'd do this one thing and then I was leaving this place and TB—forever. I'd walk down that hill like the Mayor of Chinatown. Idly I watched a young guy walking slowly up the path. Somebody's husband. Then I looked again. It was getting too dark to be sure, but—I pushed myself up and stared.

"What about the scar?" Dad was asking Rena.

"I told April—and I'll see that you do it, too, kid— just keep brushing that hair and working the right arm. And we'll put vitamin E on the wound. The scar's not worth worrying about. Believe me."

"Well, April, what do you think?" Dad asked at the very same moment that my old boyfriend, Mike, pushed open the door.

"It's what I want," I said quietly, taking Dad's hand in mine. "But let's talk later." Then I turned and grinned at Mike.

"Happy birthday tomorrow, April," he said. "Good to see you, Mr. Thorp."

"Happy birthday, Mike. Did you know we have the same birthday, Dad? He's a year older, is all. This is my new roommate, Rena, my friend Mike."

"Mike mentioned on the phone he might come by," Dad said.

"Did I interrupt something?" Mike asked, looking from one of us to the other.

"No," I said firmly. "We were talking about TB.

Same old story. We'd rather share the English toffee ice cream I bet you brought. Am I right?" I asked, pointing to the white bag in his arms.

Mike nodded. "Still your flavor?"

"I'll ring for spoons and bowls," Rena said.

After months as a no-show, what were the odds Mike would walk smack in on the biggest decision of my life? Not that I intended to ask his opinion. In that very first moment when he stood in the doorway I knew our chemistry was gone. We were too easy with each other. Mike wasn't cracking his knuckles or standing on one foot and then the other. I didn't care how my hair looked.

"I brought enough for Ravi," Mike added when Mrs. York asked how many bowls we wanted.

Ice cream instead of flowers and enough for Ravi. How's that for something or other? Flash! He's seeing someone else. He must be. So why did he come?

"That should raise Ravi's blood pressure," Dad said.

"I'll take some down to him," Mrs. York said.

"So who did you ask to the prom, Mike?"

Mike and I looked at each other for a long moment.

"Martha," he said finally, with a hangdog look.

It was my turn to nod. That figured. Martha had always liked Mike. "I thought I'd never hear from you again after my note. I'm glad you came."

"Thanks," he said with a shrug. "Like I told Mom, it's not really your fault. And it *is* our birthday."

I saw Rena and Dad raise their eyebrows at each other.

"And what did your mom say to that?" Dad asked lightly.

" 'Safe is better than sorry,' " Mike recited in a singsong voice, and we all laughed.

When we'd finished our ice cream Dad rose to go and offered Mike a ride home. Mike leaped up. "We'll talk more tomorrow, April," Dad said.

After they'd gone I turned to Rena and said, "Mike came to say goodbye. I think he has a new girlfriend."

"At least he had the courage to come and cared enough for you to want to."

"Yeah, I guess." And his coming took the edge off deciding about the surgery, too. Gave it a chance to settle in.

20

"YOU DIDN'T TELL ME I wouldn't get dinner, Rena." She and Ravi and Dad were visiting me down in the main hospital the night before my surgery, two weeks after I'd made the decision.

"You've got the rest of your life to eat," Rena said.

Ravi was pouring champagne for Dad and Rena in honor, he said, of a free India. His father had joined the other maharajahs in drafting an agreement that would soon free India from British rule.

"Our finest hour," Ravi said, his brown eyes glowing. "The end of wars."

"Maybe it's crazy but I feel like celebrating too. Tomorrow I'll be well." Well, actually I'd be a mess, but on my way out of here. Besides, if we were celebrating, Dad wouldn't remind me I could still back out.

"It's not crazy but valiant," Ravi assured me.

"Ravi, does this treaty mean it will be safe for you to go home?" Dad asked.

"You mean you can't go home?" I was shocked.

"You're on the lam?" Rena asked, raising an eyebrow.

Ravi raised both hands in that way he had, half denial, half agreement. "Some little unrest in our northern hills. Those who have grown richer under the British fear their leaving."

"Killings—" Dad began, but Ravi cut him off by raising one hand.

"Peace," he said.

"No wonder your father wanted you to stay on here for your health," Rena said.

"Rena, I am tubercular, no?"

"Your lung looked healed to me." She grinned.

"April, my beautiful one, you are worried for me?" His voice was tender.

I smiled and nodded. He looked so proud, so American in a cashmere sweater and jeans. "Some exile," I said.

A nurse came in with an instrument tray. She looked at her watch and then at us, her eyes lingering on Rena in her mother's ratty bathrobe. "I hate to be a party pooper, but I have to prep April—suppose I come back in fifteen minutes?"

"Thank you, Nurse," Dad said.

After she left, Rena and Ravi stood up. Rena put a hand on my boyfriend's arm. "You stick around. Sid Shipman said I could come down tomorrow morning. In case April's Dad here oversleeps."

"You hardly stay in bed at all," I said, to cover a sudden panic.

"Gained two pounds this week. You can't argue with success." Rena stood beside me, and suddenly she leaned over and kissed me on the forehead. "Good luck, April," she said, then turned and practically ran from the room.

My stomach churned. Why was she saying goodbye?

"She's fond of you, that's all," Dad said gently, seeing my fear.

Then it was Ravi's turn. No sneaking back after lights out tonight. Ravi stood beside me, taking my hands in his. We looked at each other silently.

Dad cleared his throat. "Maybe I'd better check at the desk and see if they've posted the surgery schedule yet. Be right back." He closed the door quietly behind him.

"Tomorrow, remember I love you," Ravi whispered, and then he kissed me, long and tenderly.

"And I love you," I said, thinking of what Dr. Clark had said when I asked about my chances tomorrow.

"You're young and healthy and we'll do our best, but there are no guarantees, April. I won't lie to you," he'd said.

"The good doctor—he will make you well," Ravi was saying confidently.

I bit my lip and looked down. "Ravi, don't come for a few days. I don't want you to see me—so ugly."

"To me, you will be beautiful and courageous as the fiercest tiger. I will come day after tomorrow."

I sighed. "No, too soon. Feed Scheherazade for me. Don't forget?"

"While she eats, we will speak of our golden lady."

Then we heard Dad in the hall, clearing his throat, an embarrassed parent trying to do the right thing by me.

Ravi kissed me quickly and opened the door, hugging Dad as they passed in the doorway.

"Well, April, you're on bright and early tomorrow. Seven-thirty A.M.," Dad said.

We looked at each other. "I'll be out of the hospital in two months," I said.

"Promise?"

Fortunately, the nurse with the instrument tray came back at that moment, because I was close to tears and Dad wasn't so dry-eyed either.

"See you tomorrow," he said.

"That's a promise." I hugged him and then he left too. I was alone with a stranger.

The nurse shaved my back and underarms, marinated me with rubbing alcohol, gave me three pills and phenobarbital, all the while talking and smiling. I had no idea what she was saying.

The next morning I lay on a gurney in the hall outside surgery, waiting my turn. The gurney was narrow and

I worried about rolling off. It seemed as if I'd been there a long time. Maybe they'd forgotten me? Rena and Dad sat on chairs next to the gurney. I wanted to tell them something but couldn't remember what. Too doped up.

"You've had her out in this hall for half an hour," I heard Rena snap at a nurse.

And suddenly I knew what I had to say. "I never even asked my mother how it felt—when I went to live with you, Dad," I said, tears running down my face.

"She knew you loved her," Dad said.

"You can phone her next week," Rena said, wiping away my tears with Kleenex.

"Just in case, would you tell her?"

Rena nodded and pressed my hand. Dad nodded too. "Just in case."

The next thing I knew I was looking up into Dr. Shipman's stern gray eyes. I lay on my side and saw Dr. Clark and two nurses also peering down at me. All wearing green caps and gowns. The operating room lights blazed. Then I couldn't see them anymore, but I could hear them talking. I heard them cutting into me but, somehow, I hardly cared.

"April, what do you feel?" Dr. Shipman asked.

"Like I'm standing on the sidewalk and someone's jackhammering." It set my teeth chattering, my chest vibrating, my ears ringing, but I didn't feel any pain.

"That's the saw. You're a great girl," Dr. Clark said.

"April's one in a million," Dr. Shipman said. "Hand me a scalpel. Clamp, Nurse. Going to the game Saturday, Bob?"

"Naaah. It'll be brutal."

"Mr. Wu said you talked about football," I mumbled. My tongue felt thick.

"What's that, honey?" Dr. Clark asked.

"Football. He said you talked—"

"Someone told April we talked about football—but it's baseball season now, kiddo."

I heard them laughing and I liked that. Everything must be okay if they were laughing. Someone held a mask to my face and said to breathe deeply, and after that I could only make out voices but no longer separate words.

It all seemed to be going on a long time and I felt cramped. I tried to move the arm I was lying on but couldn't.

"Easy does it, April. Almost done. Doctor will be closing up shop soon now," a woman said.

"April, give me five minutes. You've been great. Five minutes more."

"Okay. Ooooh," I heard myself groan, though I felt no pain.

"Give her a shot."

That was the last thing I heard.

"Dad?" He was walking alongside me, his hand covering mine. I was on the skinny gurney again and we were rolling down the hall. Dr. Shipman pushed the gurney. But my father seemed to be slipping away, sliding toward the floor, crumpled. "Hey—"

"He's fainted," Dr. Shipman said. "Smelling salts, Nurse. Mr. Thorp, pull yourself together."

"Sorry. She looks so white and pasty—"

"Dad, Dad." I tried to reach out.

"April, stay still! Mr. Thorp—okay, that's better."

But soon Dad began to slip again. This time Dr. Shipman caught him under the arms and dragged him over to a chair and sat him down. "Now stay there," he said sharply and, taking the gurney again, pushed me down the hall and into my room.

"I want my father!"

"April, don't lean over or you'll pull the stitches out."

By the time the nurses had lifted me onto the bed and propped me so that I wouldn't roll back onto the wound, my father was his usual dependable self, sitting by my bed and holding my hand.

I kept seeing Dad fainting and Dr. Shipman catching him—in a recurring dream over the blur of the next few days. My midsection would hurt and then a shot would bring dreams with colored bubbles floating through rainbows.

"She's fine, doing better than most," I heard someone tell Dad.

"Open a window. There are enough flowers in here for a funeral," I remember Dr. Shipman's booming voice saying. Ravi's roses, I thought, and couldn't remember seeing him.

Stabbing rib pain. I cried out and moaned, feeling ashamed.

"Pain on the third day after surgery is the pits." Rena's voice. "It'll pass. I brought you something to read."

Later that night I did pick up the book she'd given me. *The Sun Also Rises* by Ernest Hemingway. It was the story of a man who was impotent because of a groin wound he'd gotten in the war. Then he and this woman fall in love but they can't make love and it's all terribly heartbreaking. My scar wasn't so bad, after all. I read all night. Jake couldn't help himself, but I could.

The next morning when the nurse came in to change the dressing, I asked to see the incision.

"You're the first person who ever asked. But okay, why not? Got two mirrors?"

I handed one to her, holding mine up to catch the reflection from hers, and braced myself. What I saw was my own smooth white back, same as always, except that now it had a swollen red arc with black stitches. All these months I'd carried the image of the woman in room twelve, old and bent, with the angry red scar puckered over a bony, warty hide. I'd forgotten I was young. I sighed in relief.

"That's going to heal up without a pucker. You wait and see," the nurse said.

"Would you take this book home? Dr. Shipman will have a stroke if he sees it," I told Dad that night.

He looked at the title and laughed. "How did you like Jake?" he asked.

"You read it?"

He grinned. "Couldn't put it down."

"Me neither." But I was a little shy about discussing this story with my father, so I changed the subject. "I had the nurse show me the incision today when she changed the dressing," I said.

"And?"

"Looks better than I expected. A lot better."

"Small price for getting well, honey," Dad said.

He smiled and opened his newspaper. He looked tired and a little wrinkled. He'd been here twice a day, every day. I stretched out my hand to touch his shoulder. "Hey, thanks," I said.

"You're welcome." He grinned and looked better. My father has a really happy smile.

"Thanks for being my dad," I said.

21

By the end of the week I was back in C Ward and Rena had begun my smooth scar training.

"But it hurts. I'll pull out the stitches!"

"No, you won't, April. Sit up and brush your hair! You need to work the muscles in that arm and shoulder. If you want to swim again, brush," Rena said.

We'd settled on a hundred strokes a day. Fifty in the morning and fifty before Mrs. York came in for our backrubs, after naps. "It does feel like I'm tearing something inside."

"Adhesions! You're stretching them so you won't be a hunchback."

"Doctor, huh! You're a slave driver." But I kept brushing, with my right arm though I'm a lefty. "I hurt."

"Wait till you get my bill."

I knew Rena wasn't going to bill me, but remembering that she could shut me up.

"Smooth as a French seam," Mrs. York said a few minutes later, rolling me over and pulling up my pajama top for an alcohol rub. "Best scar I see in all my life."

"I told you so," Rena said.

"Thanks to the good Lord," added Mrs. York, rubbing alcohol briskly in circular motions over my back.

But I still remembered Nancie's phrase, "damaged goods." It was a reality check after Mrs. York's flattery.

One fluoroscope morning about a month after my surgery Dr. Shipman brought two young doctors on his rounds and showed them my incision.

"I'm proud of this one," the Great Man said.

"Great work, Doctor."

"Clean as a whistle."

"Ravi says my scar is like a tattoo, lovely as the new moon of Islam," I said.

"Wow," said one of the visiting doctors. The other chuckled.

"And how would Ravi know that?" asked Dr. Shipman coldly. I was lying on my stomach so I couldn't see his face, but I didn't like the way his hand tightened on my shoulder.

"I showed him."

"Does your father know you exhibit your incision?"

"Dad was there. I was showing them both."

Dr. Shipman sighed. "I see! Well, young lady, as long as you are a guest in my hospital, please refrain from displaying your body to young men."

"Even these young men?" I nodded at the doctors.

"Don't get smart with me, April! Doctors are different."

There were things I could have said, but I restrained myself. I didn't want to argue in front of the other doctors. Besides, wasn't he implying that looking at my scarred back was sexy? Dr. Shipman listened to my lungs a long time with the stethoscope. Finally he stood up and nodded. I gingerly rolled on my back.

"How am I?"

"Sounds good," he said grudgingly. The young doctors went on to Rena's bed, but Dr. Shipman stayed, staring down at me, tapping his mouth gently with the stethoscope, a habit he had when deciding something.

"I feel good. No dizziness, and I don't run a temperature," I said quietly.

"All right," he said abruptly. "Let's try you on ten minutes' exercise."

Exercise! I couldn't speak. I did manage a smile.

He patted my hand. "April, you'll be okay now, I think," he said quietly.

"It's like seeing a rainbow. I've waited so long."

"I know. I felt that way. too. Rainbows are okay, but take it easy, April," he said, patting my hand and then walking around the curtain toward Rena's bed.

"Hey, Rena, I'm free," I yelled. "Ten minutes' exercise."

"Whoopee!"

"Now, Rena, I expect you to ride herd on her," Dr. Shipman said, but he was laughing.

"I can watch her better if you put me on exercise, too," Rena said.

"Won't be long," he said. "Incredible recovery."

"You're a witness, April," Rena called over. Then they lowered their voices and their talk became private.

Ten minutes a day. Sometimes he took patients off exercise. But, with a little luck, ten minutes might become twenty, and then half an hour, and one sunny day soon I'd walk down that path with Dad and never come back. I'd walk the streets of San Francisco like anyone else. No one would know. I'd be free!

"That stupid bird of yours! I nearly stepped on her this time," Mary Jane said half an hour later, banging my lunch tray on the bed table.

"Well, she'd fly over your head if the store hadn't clipped her wings," I snapped. "You're jealous. Scheherazade doesn't bring you notes from Boris. Everyone else thinks she's great. Visitors look for her."

"That dumb Russian, hah!"

"So? What did he do?"

"You'd be the last to know."

"Mary Jane, if you try a little harder you can be absolutely impossible," Rena said, looking up from her book.

Mary Jane flushed and stamped out. She didn't come back with Rena's lunch until she'd delivered every other tray on the floor.

"Did you know Dr. Shipman has asked me to go into practice with him?" Rena said when Mary Jane finally came.

Mary Jane paled. Her hands shook as she picked up our water pitchers to refill them. "No, no, I didn't."

"Did he?" I asked when she'd gone.

Rena laughed and nodded. "He did, but I want variety—family practice is more my style. Mary Jane is safe from me, but it won't hurt her to worry a little."

"Yeeeah!" I said, watching Scheherazade pick her way around our door, propped open for her. She hopped up on the chair and from there to her cage and onto my bed. I took the note, folded about an inch square, from her leg and she walked up my arm and perched on my shoulder, chirping triumphantly.

" 'A thousand prayers have been offered for your health in our family temple and all have been answered,' " I read aloud. "Who told him I'm on exercise? He'll be here at two sharp, he says."

"A thousand prayers, is it? Ravi's the last of the big spenders," Rena replied.

We were supposed to take our exercise between two and five in the afternoon, and no one was allowed to dress until they had an hour a day. Dr. Shipman wanted us to walk, not primp. The neighborhood must've gotten used to seeing patients walking around in bathrobes and slippers because no one had called the police. I yearned to get half an hour so I could walk to the junior college and see kids like me. When I had an hour I'd go back to our sidewalk café.

That afternoon I was lying on top of my bed in bathrobe and slippers by two, excited and queasy, the way I used to feel before a swim meet. When Ravi hadn't come by three-thirty, I didn't know whether to be worried or hurt. "Where is he?"

Rena looked up from her book. "Either the lawyer's come or his father's calling from India," she said. "Unless, after a thousand prayers, he's shot his wad."

"What he wrote about the thousand prayers was beautiful." It was his father. I knew it. I should be using my exercise to phone my own father to tell him about it. He'd grin from ear to ear. But I wanted to walk with Ravi!

At four-ten he walked in, flushed and hurried, as if he'd run down the hall. "Congratulations, my beautiful," he said. Something was wrong.

"What's up?" I asked.

"April thought you'd left for Kashmir," said Rena.

"My father says he is coming to visit me—next week, perhaps." Ravi didn't sound pleased.

"Is he in this country?" asked Rena.

"At present, he is still at home."

"Is he coming to take you home?" I asked, my stomach flip-flopping. What would I do?

"No."

"Why, then?" Rena asked.

"Business," said Ravi firmly. "But it is the lovely summer day—no?—and April and I have waited so long to walk outside together."

"I'll be lucky to get down the hall and back in ten minutes."

Ravi was luring my parakeet onto his hand and into the cage, talking softly to her.

"Now, come," he said, offering his arm. "You want your mistress to walk, do you not, birdie? April, my beautiful, ten minutes starts when we are in the sunshine, no?"

My legs buckled just thinking about walking down the hall. Could I do this?

I made it. Ravi held open the steel door and we stepped out. After so much hospital disinfectant, I'd forgotten what sunshine smelled like. I inhaled the odor of drying grass and eucalyptus trees from the hillside behind us. The smell of roses! The sun soothed my face and hands. I closed my eyes and lifted my face. The soft warmth felt like a blessing. "Pinch me, Ravi, so I'll know it's for real."

"Soon you'll be running all over the countryside," he said, kissing my hand.

"And swimming."

"And we can go dancing," Ravi said.

"It's almost eight months since I've felt sunshine, basked in the sun. Except for that day at the dentist."

"Shall we promenade, my beloved?"

We walked slowly around the patio, stopping to

touch a dazzling red rhododendron and to pick a California poppy.

"Our state flower. And my favorite." I twirled the poppy stem, delighting in the glossy orange petals, the ferny leaves.

"Ah, yes? I shall have the florist send some."

"I love your roses," I said, though they'd gotten pretty predictable. The poppy was all instinct, answering the first rains. "Oh, hooray! Hooray! I'm free!"

But Ravi glanced at his watch. My freedom was pretty limited. We turned and opened the heavy doors and walked back down the hall, hand in hand. Let people gossip.

I was surprised to find myself sweating by the time we got back to my room. And short of breath as I climbed back into bed. Maybe I was still sick? "Rena, I brought you a poppy. But I'm too exhausted to bring it over. Do you think I pulled something?"

Rena laughed. "After eight months penned up on that bed like a rabbit, it amazes me that you can still walk. Not to worry. Every day will get easier."

"Thanks." So I was okay. I fell asleep and woke only when Dad and the supper tray arrived simultaneously. "I'm on exercise," I said, laughing and clapping my hands.

"Congratulations." He spoke quietly, but his warm grin was everything I'd hoped for.

———

After lights out that night Ravi slipped into our room, his first after-hours visit since my operation. He came over to my bed, putting his arms around me, and kissed me long and tenderly.

"We must talk," he said, kissing me again.

"All right."

"We must talk," he said fiercely, as if I'd objected.

"All right."

"My father . . ." He laid his cheek against mine, and for a moment, I thought he'd fallen asleep, but then he took hold of my shoulders and stood staring at me by the light from the moon.

"We must be brave, my love," he said.

"Oh, why?" I wondered if Rena was listening.

"My father. I say to him today that you are on exercise, almost well. That we are in love."

"Oh, dear." He couldn't think I'd go off to India—not now, without Dad? Without Dr. Shipman? Without finishing high school?

"Ooooh, my heart is breaking."

"What did your father say, Ravi?"

"We want to marry, I say to him."

"But—"

"My father, he say, alas, but he has already betrothed me for seven months to a Punjabi girl whose acquaintance I have yet to make. I know only that she is beautiful. I must marry for our family, he says."

"What?" I sat straight up and held him at arm's length. "You're kidding."

"No, my darling."

"Your father chooses who you marry?"

"In my country it is the custom."

"Someone you've never even met?"

For once Ravi had nothing to say. He only nodded, trying to move closer.

"No," I said, and to my horror, started crying. "And your father's never even met me." I sobbed.

I could hear the night nurse in the hall. "Boris isn't on tonight. You'd better go," I whispered.

"I don't care."

"Well, I do. Go. We'll talk tomorrow." The nurse was getting closer. "Now! She's in the room next door. Now—go." All I wanted was to have him out of my room.

"But I love you."

Rena's voice made us both jump.

"Invite us to the wedding. Now, get out of here, Ravi, or you'll get her taken off exercise."

He fled.

Rena said nothing more. I cried.

"Rena, are you awake?" I asked finally.

"Fat chance of sleeping."

"How can Ravi know she's beautiful if he's never heard of her until today?"

"The lawyer probably brought pictures months ago."

"That's what I think. So he didn't find out today?"

"Maybe for sure, today."

"He lied to me."

"Oh, come on, April. Were you planning on marrying Ravi and moving to India?"

"He should have told me as soon as he knew."

"When? During your last hemorrhage or when you were waiting for surgery?"

"I'll never trust him again."

"Just as well. Now, let's get some sleep, kid."

Sleep? Not likely. How could he marry someone he'd never even met? How could anyone? But Rena said ninety-five percent of Indians did. Not me! I'd run away.

Soon I got to thinking that in all the fifty rooms of our hospital, only Ravi and I were awake. Even Rena's breathing had become heavy and regular. I felt all that breathing, all that restless dreaming, and gradually, despite everything, I found myself drifting off, the loss of my Indian prince whispering at the edge of sleep.

22

"YOU CAN ALWAYS run off and elope," Rena suggested early the next morning.

"I'd be back here in three months. Hemorrhaging while Mary Jane laughed. I've got other plans."

"No maharani training?"

I managed a rueful laugh. It was dawn, one of those golden summer dawns rising like a lovely dream of day. I stretched and yawned. The only real plan I had was getting out of here. I'd slept only fitfully, thinking most of the night. I thought of Nancie and how she'd wanted to tell Dino there were no hard feelings because they had had so much happiness. I felt the same way, though it still stuck in my craw that Ravi had lied. His father must be worse than Genghis Khan. I was not cut out to be his daughter-in-law. Even if Ravi had known about this "so very beautiful" fiancée for a while, so what? He'd helped me through surgery. Loved me when it counted. How many guys would have treated me like a princess when I was spitting blood? Mike had freaked out when I'd only started coughing. Even Dad had fainted when I was coming back from surgery.

"The only thing," I said, thinking aloud. "And this really gets to me—it's as if Ravi'll be in prince training from now on. Like he was that day with the lawyer. You know, Rena?"

"His betrothal sets it in concrete, hmmm? Getting well. Marriage. Kids. Work."

"Yeeeah. What happened to living each day? What happened to Cambridge?"

"Cambridge is part of princely training these days. And I can't imagine Ravi settling down quite yet, can you?"

"I don't know."

Ravi arrived promptly at two o'clock. Showered, shaved, and smelling of that wonderful musky cologne. For once, he said nothing, waiting for a cue.

I grinned. "It's okay. Relax."

"What are we to do?" he asked then, with that sweet Ravi grin and his hands spread palms up, imploring the gods.

"Go for a walk," I said, with a significant glance at Rena's closed curtain.

"For my father—life is family honor," Ravi began as we pushed through the heavy doors onto the patio.

I breathed deeply, smelling roses, taking time to digest the hint that I wasn't a bride who brought honor. "My father would never allow me to marry anyone before I finish college," I said finally to rescue my pride, implying Dad had laid down the law, which he'd never dream of doing. He'd always trusted me.

"Yes, your father rejected my offer of marriage," Ravi said sadly. But I thought I detected relief in his voice.

"Hmmm, he said only a literary friendship," I agreed.

"But our love?"

I kissed him and then stepped back, holding both his hands. "Our love's here," I said. "I'll always remember the year of my Indian prince, Ravi."

"And I will love you, my beautiful one, every day of my life."

"Our secret," I murmured, calling up disturbing visions of Ravi kissing his bride and thinking of me. It would serve her right. My mother had written last week, saying a romantic friendship with Ravi was lovely but *baby, please remember you won't be going to India. Don't sound so serious.* Okay, Mom. Right again.

We walked quietly for a few minutes and then I turned toward the door. Time to go back. Ravi drew me close.

"And our year is not yet over," he whispered. "The best is yet to come. You'll see, my beautiful April. You'll see."

I smiled. "I'm waiting."

———

As it turned out, we had almost two months before Ravi's father came for him. One border rebellion after another that summer of 1946 delayed the maharajah's departure from India. Rena, Dad and I kept finding his name in the newspaper. It was all very exciting.

Meanwhile, Ravi and I knew we were on borrowed time. We made a pact not to mention his engagement because I'd explode and we hadn't the time to waste fighting. We were desperate to cherish every day. Fortunately, Dr. Shipman kept increasing my exercise.

The day I got forty minutes we left the hospital grounds and walked over toward the junior college. Ravi wore his caftan and I wore the one he had given me because it felt more acceptable on the street than a red wool bathrobe, and I needed an hour's exercise before I could dress. So we strolled along like two desert sheiks.

A girl on a bicycle glanced at me, grinned and waved, and pedaled on.

"Maybe she thinks we're sacred cows," I said, knowing he'd love thinking of us being like the sacred white cows running wild over India.

"I told you people are used to us," Ravi said.

"That girl on the bike didn't even stare."

"And what do you think? She's worrying about caftans or getting a sweetheart herself when she sees us so happy together?"

"I should make you wear a photograph of your betrothed around your neck. Oops! Sorry."

Ravi turned to me and took both my hands. His face

was flushed and sad. "Listen, April. Father says I do not marry for four years—after I have received my Cambridge University degree. So much will happen in my poor country before that. This marriage—perhaps go poof! Besides, how can you worry when I have never met this lady?"

"You are engaged, aren't you?"

Ravi shrugged and smiled, dismissing and admitting his engagement at the same time.

"Why don't you stand up to your father and say no?"

He held up his hand in the gesture of peace, but I could see anger in his smoldering eyes. "It is the way of all India. All my family. You do not understand us here. But have we so many days, we can fight?"

His voice dropped. He purred the last words. We'd made a mum's-the-word deal. These days were ours. And all the rest were hers?

"No, we don't."

Ravi pursed his lips. He didn't trust me.

"I'm jealous, okay?" I smiled and took his hand.

He sighed and shook himself like a puppy. It was a gesture Ravi used for what he called "restoring unity."

"So my beautiful one?" He spread his arms wide, but his expression was still wary.

"Ravi, I'm just curious about her. Aren't you?"

His eyes narrowed. "I dream only of you. See!" He flipped open his wallet to a picture he'd taken my first day on exercise. "And if you're so curious, come to India and see her for yourself."

"I would come to ride elephants and stalk tigers. But your betrothed might throw gasoline on me and light the match."

"Ah, no, she is Brahmin and could not use violence."

"Oh, well, in that case, sure." Dad had emptied his bank account for my surgery. I'd be lucky to make it to college, let alone India, and if there was extra money he'd send it to Mom. But try to make Ravi understand being broke. "Hey, let's go on the college grounds. We can have a Coke and people-watch."

Ravi looked at his watch and raised an eyebrow.

"I'm due back in twenty minutes, right? No one's keeping time. Dear Mary Jane is off today."

"We said we'd be back."

"You've got two hours!"

Ravi shook his head and stood as if he'd put down roots.

"Oh, come on! I need an adventure! I'm tired of waking up to a chorus of coughing, sick of two A.M. temperature checks. Come on!"

"An adventure?" Ravi echoed dubiously.

"You've never been in an American college, have you!"

Ravi shrugged.

I turned abruptly and walked on ahead. I was well. I needed to be with kids like me. I wanted to be me again, not the sick girl.

Ravi caught up with me and took my hand. "All right, adventure," he said. A little smile tugged at the corners of his mouth and then took over his whole face, so sunny and delightful that I leaned over and kissed him.

Ahead of us, the campus spread over the crest of a knoll, oaks and weeping willows and sweeping lawns. The buildings looked Spanish, white stucco with tile roofs. Except for the fact that it wasn't walled, the college might have been one of the California missions. And behind it rose Mount Tamalpais, my mountain.

"What's that?" Ravi asked as we reached the lawn, pointing to an old wooden barn set back in a hollow, between eucalyptus and a stand of pine.

"Let's go see!" I dropped his hand and ran down the grassy slope, waving my arms. I wanted to lie down and roll in the grass, to turn cartwheels, walk on my hands, fly. I wanted to cover the barn with writing and sing to the sun.

"Bring on the world," I called.

A sudden stab of pain in my chest made me stop to catch my breath and I stood there panting and aching, tears in my eyes, when Ravi caught up to me.

"Next month you run, not yet," he said, putting an arm around my heaving shoulders. "As Boris would say, where is the fire?"

"I want to see inside." The pain was easing.

"Someone will shoot us for trespassing."

"Hah!"

The barn door squeaked as I pulled it open and peered inside, half blinded by sunlight.

"Come on in, beautiful, the water's fine." I jumped and then saw a big redheaded guy sitting at an easel just inside the door. He was grinning and beckoning.

"Uh-oh," I whispered.

"Good afternoon," Ravi said uncertainly.

"Come on in," answered the smiling hunk of a man. "Are you from the hospital?"

We nodded.

"Obviously," I added. "Are you in class?"

"Semester's about over, but here at the art barn we're still finishing up. Celebrating, really. A painting of mine just took a first prize. Congratulate me! Come on. I'll give you the grand tour."

"Great!" My voice echoed in the rafters, twenty feet up. Skylights focused sun like spotlights over the dark wooden floors and the easels. There was a potters' corner with three wheels and a kiln, and there were racks of drying pots in various stages of glazing. Half a dozen students were working, but the other easels had smocks draped over a corner, as if the artist had gone out for a sandwich. The students were drawing a model, a muscular young man wearing nothing but a precarious jockstrap. The barn smelled of coffee and fresh paint and hummed with talk and soft laughter.

"This is the most wonderful place I've seen in my whole life," I said. "If I could—"

"Well, you haven't been around much lately, I reckon," replied our new friend, regarding me with intense blue eyes. I couldn't help smiling back at him.

"Like a temple workshop but—happier," Ravi added, taking my hand firmly.

"Come on out back and have a drink and tell me about yourselves. By the way, name's John, Plain John."

"This is Ravi and I'm April. Glad to meet you, John." John and I laughed a little. Ravi frowned.

We followed Plain John across the barn. Students looked up and smiled. One girl asked if she could sketch Ravi in his caftan, a sheik straight off the desert was what she called him.

"Maybe for ten minutes? I would be honored." Ravi smiled and bowed. She worked rapidly, producing a line drawing that caught the warmth in his brown eyes and the fine structure of his face, even his eagerness. When she was done she ripped the sketch off her drawing board and handed it to me.

"It's really him," I said.

"To remember him by," she said softly.

How did she know he'd be leaving? It was all I could do to smile and thank her. I felt chilled and dizzy, as if Ravi had already gone.

But I shook myself out of that and followed the two men. We sat under a willow outside the back door of the barn. We snapped open root beers and drank from the cans, trading personal histories. Probably everyday stuff to the big redhead, but I felt as if I'd died and gone to heaven. Plain John said he'd grown up on a farm outside Petaluma and aimed to paint like Van

Gogh. He thought living in the hospital sounded romantic and melancholy and wanted to come visit us.

"Sure, any afternoon after two-thirty," I said.

"Well, we have our exercise and it's not always convenient." There was reservation in Ravi's voice.

"Man, I'm adaptable. I'll sketch someone until you show up."

"You think of us as subjects?"

"No, friend. I think of you as a guy who had the luck to get off the career train for a spell."

"Little does he know." Ravi stopped me from saying more with a look.

"April, we must go!"

"I turn into a pumpkin if I'm late, but come see me anyhow," I invited John as warmly as I could, as Ravi hurried us off.

"This is where I'm going to college. This is it! I'll tell Dad tonight," I said as we walked back up the hill.

"You flirted with him!" Ravi was outraged.

"Oh, wasn't it fun? Isn't it fun having something to be jealous about? Isn't it?"

Ravi didn't answer, but I could see he was thinking it over, and when I took his arm, he covered my hand with his. We walked on in companionable silence.

"Remember, only I love you," he said, opening our hospital door.

I smiled. But I was thinking of the redhead who'd won a prize and the students drawing at those easels. Did they have any idea how lucky they were, and was it possible that—soon—I might join them? And if Nancie hadn't urged me to go ahead, would I have had the surgery? I touched her pearl earrings, which I wore always, with gratitude.

"Now, we must slip into our beds without arousing suspicion," Ravi warned me as we hurried down the hall.

I was an hour late, possibly the first patient in the history of the hospital to be an hour late and get away with it. It felt good to lie back as I got into bed.

"Just remember that Icarus melted his wings when he flew too close to the sun," Rena said softly.

I grinned and, leaning over toward her bed, handed her the drawing of Ravi.

23

R AVI'S FATHER finally arrived on the Fourth of
July, and it seemed to me that all the fireworks ex-
ploded in his honor. He towered well above six feet and
looked as if he'd spent a lifetime receiving twenty-one-
gun salutes.

The maharajah reminded me of Dr. Shipman. Both
men could reduce a roomful of people to silence in five
minutes just by looking them over and raising one eyebrow. Ravi trailed behind and looked mortified.

Dad and I were invited out to dinner with Ravi and
his father in what had to be the fanciest Indian restaurant in the world, with golden drapes and Kashmir rugs
and real silver and orchid bouquets on white table-
cloths. There was a spectacular view of the bay and
Mount Tamalpais. If I ignored the other diners and sat
listening to the sitar player and looking out over the
water I could imagine we were in Bombay. We might
as well have asked to go to Bombay for all the rules Dr.

Shipman had laid down before he'd let me leave the hospital for the evening.

Anyhow, we sat there surrounded by turbaned waiters offering spicy hors d'oeuvres. Ravi smiled nervously at Dad and me, drinking tea, strangely subdued. I couldn't help wondering what we were all doing there together.

I didn't know what to say to any maharajah, let alone one who didn't want me for a daughter-in-law. Ravi's father obviously felt that feeding us was more than enough effort on his part. That left Dad to try to start a conversation. Luckily he was never at a loss if someone interested him, and Ravi's father did.

"We've been following your negotiations in the newspaper, sir. Will the British leave India?"

"Ah, have you? Yes, certainly they will go. Eagerly."

"When?"

"Soon, like rats deserting a sinking ship, leaving us with partition, I'm afraid." The maharajah crooked his finger for a waiter. Two responded instantly. "We're ready to order now," he told them.

That put me in a panic, since I hadn't even looked at the menu. I ordered chicken curry because it was first on the list. Then everyone else ordered vegetarian curries, which made me feel carnivorous. I'd forgotten his father would be a vegetarian, of course, being Hindu.

Ravi and his father must have had some kind of argument. The maharajah kept glancing over at his son and frowning. Ravi glared back.

"But you've worked to get the British to leave all my life," Ravi said.

"Certainly, but gradually, leaving us one country."

"How do you think partition will work, Your Highness?" Dad asked after the waiter took our orders.

"It will be a disaster."

Dad pursed his lips. "How so?"

The maharajah shrugged and said nothing. I could see Dad's patience was wearing thin.

"Ravi gives my roommate and me lessons in Indian history. Tell your dad."

"April's roommate is the doctor who would like to make your acquaintance," Ravi said. His voice was calm and steady, but there was still that angry edge to it. What was going on?

"I'll never forget hearing what it's like to live on a houseboat in Kashmir." I couldn't stop chattering.

"What is it like?" asked the maharajah, turning to me.

My mind blanked. I couldn't remember. Not one word. I looked across the table, but Ravi was staring out at the bay. His father watched me intently.

"Oh—oh," I stammered. "It's beautiful. Shopkeepers come on board—every morning—selling flowers and vegetables and beautiful shawls. And at night you're lulled to sleep by the water, right, Ravi?" My voice rose on his name and he looked up, miserable. I kicked him under the table.

"Ah, yes, you bring back my poor words with grace," he said with a sudden smile.

His father pursed his lips and said nothing.

Four turbaned waiters set down trays of spicy curries on our table. My favorite food. Dad raised his teacup to propose a toast. "To the good health of our children," he said.

The maharajah raised his cup and nodded. "Yes, to their continued good health." Then, after a sigh, he continued. "Are you aware, sir, that my son has bought your daughter an airline ticket to India?"

Dad turned to me with a surprised look. "One-way or round-trip?" he asked.

"Hey, I don't know a thing about this," I said, flushing, remembering that Ravi had said I should visit India and see his fiancée. It was the day we had met Plain John at the college.

"Ah, come now," said the maharajah.

"She doesn't know! You insult my friend," Ravi said, standing. "It was to be a surprise. Round trip," he added, smiling at Dad and sitting again. "A so small token of our literary friendship."

"My son is to be betrothed on his return to India."

"Yes, we have congratulated him. May I also congratulate you, Your Highness," replied Dad, the beginnings of a smile tugging at his mouth.

"Then—"

"Exactly," said Dad.

"But you can see how improper, under the circumstances, this visit must be considered. The free ways of your great country are not those of my poor land." The maharajah cleared his throat, frowning, then dropped his eyes under Dad's fierce look.

"The trip has not been offered to April, nor will it be accepted. Therefore, the matter rests between you and your son, sir. Now, please——" Dad held up his hand in Ravi's peace gesture.

Ravi's father rose, pushing back his chair.

"Father, people are staring," Ravi said.

"My son also admitted that he made a certain ill-considered promise in a letter to you, sir."

"I told you he refused me, Father. You are suffering for no reason."

"The letter might still stand in a court of law."

Ravi flushed and held his face in his hands. What letter? The one about visiting me to see if we should prove mutually compatible for marriage? Ravi knew his father better than to tell him that! Unless he didn't want to get married! If I showed up in India, would her family break the engagement? I grinned at Ravi, and he gave me a look of such tenderness that I could feel the heat rise in my cheeks.

"I threw that away the day it arrived," snapped Dad, setting down his fork, laying his napkin beside his plate, nodding at me and gesturing for the waiter. "This has been enlightening—but I'd better get my daughter back to the hospital."

Well, the maharajah fairly ran over to the waiter.

"He'd lose face if you paid," Ravi said.

"No doubt. Thank you so much, Ravi. Please pay our respects to your father. Let's go, April." Dad laid his hand for a moment on Ravi's shoulder, smiled at him, then turned and walked away.

Ravi looked up. "I tried to stop this," he said quietly.

I nodded, cast a longing look at my delicious dinner, hardly touched, then got up and followed Dad, trying to walk like a princess as we crossed the palatial room.

I didn't see Ravi the next day, nor the day after, because he was in San Francisco shopping with his father. He bowed at my feet and begged me to forgive him, according to his note. Rena said the maharajah was keeping Ravi under lock and key because he was afraid we'd elope, and I'd better consider the night before last our goodbye. I'd begun to fear she was right when another note asked me to save my next exercise period for him, who loved me. He said he'd seen me walking with Plain John.

"April has one hour, Ravi. This is no country club, you know," Mary Jane snapped, holding up her pudgy forefinger as she closed the hall door behind us the next afternoon.

"She must have seen the taxi," Ravi whispered.

"She's jealous," I replied, awed myself by the taxi.

"She should allow herself happiness with Boris."

"She calls him 'that Russian.' " We smiled at each other.

Once in the cab, Ravi put his arm around me, and I laid my head on his shoulder. My heart beat faster. I wanted him to kiss me. Never mind his father, never mind the fiancée. We were happy together.

"And we have proved compatible," he said fiercely, tracing the outlines of my eyes, mouth, jaw, forehead as if he were committing my face to memory. "Guess where we're going, beautiful one?"

"Does it matter?" All I wanted was to be alone, rid of the taxi driver watching us in his rearview mirror.

Ravi nodded, kissing my hand.

Then we began to climb into the hills and I knew. "Mount Tamalpais. Oh, thank you!" I cranked down the window and breathed deeply of pine and redwood.

"We will walk on your mountain."

I'd never told Ravi how I yearned to walk again on the mountain I'd watched from my bed month after month, but apparently he knew. "You must be a mind reader," I murmured, putting my arms around him and holding tight. "Ravi, is it any wonder I love you?"

"None at all."

A few minutes later I stood looking down at the hospital and the ribbon of road leading to the college while Ravi paid the driver. "They look like buildings from a Monopoly game," I told Ravi when he returned.

"Why attend this college so close to the hospital?" he

asked so sadly that I turned and kissed him. The power of our kiss astonished us both and we stood there, clinging, taken by surprise, in love and despair.

"When do you leave?"

"Tomorrow." He groaned.

"Not tomorrow!" We held each other. Tomorrow night he'd be halfway around the world. I'd always known parting was inevitable—but not tomorrow. Not yet! "I might never see you again! Never, ever in all the years of my life. How can we bear it?"

"I have been so happy with you, happier than ever in this life." Ravi kissed me again, even more passionately than before. "I bask in the radiance of your face."

"Only radiant with you."

"Only with me."

We clung. We held each other, silently passing our hands along each other's bodies, longing as I'd never longed before. I caught Ravi's hand and kissed it. I knew how Rena and Paul felt. I gently pushed him away. "A literary friendship," I whispered.

Ravi looked deeply into my eyes.

"Let's walk on my mountain."

Ravi sighed deeply, but we walked, kissing as we went.

"Tomorrow we part forever."

"My darling April, no, not forever," Ravi said, wrapping me in his arms again.

But I knew better. Walking gave me a little time to feel tired, made me afraid of getting sick again. Tomorrow he'd leave me, and the day after, he'd meet his fiancée. His father's choice, I kept reminding myself as Ravi began to lay plans for us.

"I'll have to see our good doctor once, maybe twice each year. We will have a week together each time, beloved."

"Hmmmm."

"Maybe the doctor needs to see me even more."

"Maybe there are doctors in India."

"Then why am I here?"

I couldn't answer that one.

"I am not the same man after loving you—after our hospital life together. I think through your eyes," he said.

"I know." It was true. I only had to wonder what Ravi would think about—anything—and call up the love in his eyes and, yes, I would think through his eyes as well as my own. "I love you," I said, pointing to the dust of the returning taxi, speeding up the wooded road to reclaim us, and burst into tears.

When Ravi and his father left for India the next afternoon, I stood by my window waving. I would be leaving soon too, but would I ever have another love as understanding and romantic? A boyfriend who thought of a scar as a sacred crescent moon? Ravi was my prince and my best friend. These tears were his tribute.

"Ra-vi. Ra-vi," chirped Scheherazade.

Outside the building he turned and we looked at each other. "Goodbye, goodbye," I called.

"Until we meet again," Ravi shouted, loudly enough so the entire floor heard him and the maharajah turned and frowned.

Rena sighed. "Why not dress and then take a little rest?" she said when he'd gone.

Yes. Plain John, the tall redhead who intended to paint like Van Gogh, would be coming in an hour to take exercise with me. But—I only wanted Ravi.

24

A MONTH LATER, on a sunny afternoon much like the one when I had first come to the hospital almost a year ago, it was my turn to go home. I sat in a chair by Rena's bed waiting for Dad.

"With you and Ravi gone, I might as well go home too. It's no fun anymore," she said.

"And I'm jealous of your new roommate already. I'll be so lonely without you, Rena."

"Don't you dare sulk, April! Keep brushing your hair so you'll look good in a bathing suit. Paul and I will be knocking on your door before you know it."

I took a deep breath to keep from disgracing myself by crying. Our door opened and Mary Jane came in to change the water pitchers.

"Well, April, don't do anything crazy that lands you back here," Mary Jane said in her usual maddening way. But then she surprised me. She set down Rena's water and lightly placed one finger on each of Nancie's pearl earrings hanging from my ears.

"We'll never forget her, will we?"

"Never in all our lives," I said.

Mary Jane nodded, her blue eyes exacting my promise. Then she turned and walked out with the empty pitchers, her crepe soles making the soft catchy sound I'd dreaded for so long.

"Well, I'll be damned," Rena said with a smile.

Oh, Nancie, you would have laughed, I thought.

Then Mrs. York came in with Dad. She wrapped her arms around me, and we each shed a few tears as she kept asking God to take care of me.

Dad took Scheherazade's cage in one hand and my suitcase in the other.

"Ready, April?" he asked with a grin.

I sat there, looking at him.

"We'll come back to visit," he said gently.

Mrs. York, Rena and I sighed in unison.

"Okay, in that case, I'll see you later," I said, standing and kissing Mrs. York on her soft cheek.

"Oh, Rena," I said, hugging her and then walking out of C Ward as Dad held the door.

For the last time as a patient, I walked down the hillside path isolating tuberculars from the world. I was going home. I was well. The sun glowed on my face as I turned back and waved to Rena and Mrs. York and even Mary Jane. On my wrist three gold bracelets jingled, each inscribed "From Ravi with love." I knew there would be some patients whose feet were walking in their beds, as mine had walked with the Mayor of Chinatown when he left us. I blew them kisses.

"It's all over, April. I'm taking you home at last," Dad said with his big lopsided grin, swinging Scheherazade in her Victorian cage.

"Home, home," chirped the parakeet.

I could only nod. How many times had I dreamed of this moment, the happiest day of my life? So why did I feel so choked up? My wings felt as clipped as Scheherazade's. Of course, I was only allowed to be up half a day and had to report back to Dr. Shipman every other week "for a gradual transition." I'd have a home teacher to help me finish high school quickly so I could go on to college next semester. I'd hoped to go back to my old high school, but half my friends, including Mike, had already graduated.

No, going home wasn't making me sad, but— maybe—the hospital had come to feel like home. Would I ever again have a friend as close as Nancie? I didn't even have a photo of her, I thought with a gasp. Or of anyone else—just Ravi. I'd never seen anyone with a camera, except Ravi once. Didn't we think we'd want to remember? Didn't we think we'd survive?

"Dad, when we come back to visit can we take a photo of Rena? And Mrs. York and Boris? We'll stay until the evening shift to see Boris, too. He'll sure be mad when he gets here today and I'm gone."

"Sure. If you don't behave I'll do a six-by-eight-foot enlargement of Mary Jane, too."

I'd send copies to Ravi. There'd never be another Ravi, my sweet prince in far-off India, the land of tigers and marriages arranged with strangers. He was marrying a stranger, even though we'd gotten so close we knew what the other was going to think before he even thought it! I'd probably end up an old maid because he'd spoiled me for any other guy.

Dad must have felt my sadness, because he took my arm and helped me into the car without a word. We passed the college, Spanish buildings with lawns and weeping willows sweeping down to an old wooden art barn.

"That's where I'm going to school," I said, brightening. "Plain John is coming to visit me next Tuesday."

"Why not? The world's your oyster now, April," Dad said.

Then we were on the Golden Gate Bridge. Across the blue water San Francisco shimmered in the late-afternoon sunlight, mysterious and yet familiar. My heart quickened. I began to get excited by all we were seeing.

"I'd forgotten—oh, we are going home. Home, Dad!"

"You betcha."

As we turned onto our block on Sacramento Street, I heard the long, low chanting from Temple Emmanuel on the corner. It must be five already, time for synagogue, I thought. Neighbors were out on the street, clustered in front of the Russian grocery across from our flat, one old lady calling in Russian to two women sitting on the steps next door. Guys about my age were playing basketball in the schoolyard.

"It hasn't changed at all. It's like I've been in a time warp," I said, trying to take everything in, the happy jumble of sounds. I kept looking around, hungry for the faces and colors. A streetcar stopped on the corner and people with packages came tumbling off, smiling, promising to meet again tomorrow.

I saw neighbors I hadn't seen for so long, nor even thought about. The summer sun was slanting low over rooftops, shadowing their faces. Would they welcome me or keep their distance? Would I be April or that girl with TB? Would they be afraid of me?

"I can't talk to anyone yet," I whispered as Dad parked our car in the garage. "Please."

"Okay. Tomorrow, then. You'll find some changes."

I nodded. I couldn't care about changes here yet. Let me settle in. I wanted to ask Dad what the neighbors said about me coming home. But maybe it was better to take one thing at a time, as Mom had suggested when I'd phoned to tell her I was going home.

We climbed the stairs to our old flat, and as Dad opened the door, the first thing I saw was a big bowl of long-stemmed red roses on the hall table.

"Ravi?"

"He doesn't give up easily," Dad said with a smile.

"Ra-vi, Ra-vi," chirped Scheherazade.

I picked up an envelope that had come with the flowers and opened it, reading eagerly. "Ravi has an appointment with Dr. Shipman next year on March twentieth and hopes you and I will join him that evening for an Indian dinner," I said.

Dad and I looked at each other and grinned. Then he said what we were both thinking.

"That's some literary friendship!"

"March twentieth," I said, thinking it over. "I'll be in my second semester of college by then. And maybe he'll come over from Cambridge University. We'll have a lot to talk about, that's for sure. And you're invited, too."

Dad smiled. "We'll see what's on my social calendar for next March."

We walked on through the apartment and automatically sat down at our old places at the kitchen table, overlooking our back garden. I'd grown up at this table, eating, doing homework, reading, playing checkers, talking over the day with Dad. It felt good to be back.

"Hey, I'm well and you're home from the war," I said. The words felt as if they were burbling all through me. They felt like joy.

Dad only nodded, but his grin said it all.

AFTERWORD

As a young girl I was a patient in a tuberculosis hospital in Ross, California, for three years. World War II had ended and my father had come home from the army. My beautiful roommate Nancie had the most wonderful laugh, but unfortunately she and other friends did die. Our visit to the crematorium was borrowed from my friend Jean in another hospital. Nancie's boyfriend married, but I invented his personality and that of his mother to make a better story and show the way healthy people treated us. After Nancie died, I did have a roommate who was a friendly genius. Dr. Sidney Shipman always wanted me to write about him and finally I have.

How about Ravi? There was a maharajah's son from northern India who courted me. He lacked Ravi's gentle sense of humor but had his wisdom. He sent me roses and chocolates. He said my scar was like a crescent moon. We shared discussions of the tumultuous struggles for Indian freedom, though he was back in India when independence was declared in 1947. Knowing India's history has helped me understand struggles for independence around the world. We shared our lives. However, within six months of leaving the hospital we were each engaged to someone else.

Today, three million people in the world die of tuberculosis every year. Fortunately, most patients in this country no longer spend years in bed but are treated with drugs. However, in poorer countries bed rest like mine is still the cure.

ELLA THORP ELLIS

Opposite: The author's senior class picture, taken the month of her diagnosis.